Hardback - ISBN: 978-1-923567-18-4
Paperback - ISBN: 978-1-923567-19-1
eBook - ISBN: 978-1-923567-20-7

Cover design by Holly Symons
First Edition

For More, Please Visit
HollySymons.com.au

Aurelya & Loki

The Gate That Broke the Realms

The Book Loki Wasn't Supposed to Be In

The Realm Shatter Saga

(Book One: The Gate That Broke the Realms)

(Book Two: The Realm of Roots)

(Book Three: The Realm of Echoes)

BONUS CONTENT

Flameborn Presents: Tales Too Weird to Fit in Properly

Chapter One: Odin, The Rope, and the Ridiculous Tree Day

Starring: Aurelya, Loki, a very confused squirrel, and a god who thinks dramatic suffering equals wisdom.

[Scene: The Base of Yggdrasil – Day One of Odin's "Great Sacrifice"]

The wind was having a moment. Dramatic gusts swirled leaves, whispered secrets, and very nearly unbuckled Odin's cloak. He adjusted it, solemn, towering under the colossal branches of Yggdrasil.

Odin took a long, brooding breath.
"This… is the day I surrender myself to the void to gain ultimate wisdom."
He looked around. No audience.
Except for a confused squirrel halfway up the tree.

"I hung for nine days, suspended between life and death!" Odin bellowed to nobody in particular, arms outstretched.

"You're yelling at a rodent," came a voice like

mischief wrapped in silk.
Loki stepped out from behind the trunk, biting
into an apple that definitely wasn't his.
"What, no crowd? No harpist?" He glanced up.
"No ravens even? Tough gig."

"This is sacred," Odin muttered, tying a rope
around his waist in what could only be described
as a theatrical tangle.
"I give myself to the World Tree."

Loki squinted.
"You're hanging yourself… from the thing you're
trying to impress? Bit clingy."

Odin ignored him.
He slung the rope over a high branch, grunted,
and hoisted himself up with all the grace of a
very determined walrus. His sword clattered to
the ground.

"WISDOM! KNOWLEDGE! SACRIFICE!" Odin
declared again as he dangled awkwardly, upside-
down.
The squirrel stared. So did Loki.

"By the realms, he's actually doing it," Loki said,
half-laughing, half-impressed.
Then a hum.

A pulse under the bark.

Loki's smile twitched.

From the sap, something stirred.
[Cut to: Somewhere deeper, unseen – the core of
Yggdrasil]

Aurelya was born of starlight and sap, curled in a
sphere of glowing golden resin.
Eyes closed.
Crown already present.
Wings folded within her back like dormant
constellations.

Odin, unknowingly, had triggered her arrival. But
the roots kept their secrets.

[Later that same day – Realm walker's Clearing]

Loki sat beneath a different branch, drawing
shapes in the dirt with a stick. The squirrel now
sat beside him. They'd reached a strange truce.

Then it happened.
A crackle.
A shimmer.
Aurelya appeared like light unravelling from silk

gold and quiet fire.
She blinked, tilted her head.

"Are you the one who keeps shouting?"
Loki froze.
The squirrel fainted.

"...You're not from any realm I know," Loki said,
slowly standing.
"What are you?"

She looked toward the World Tree, where Odin
now hung snoring (or possibly in meditative
agony, it was hard to tell).
Her voice was serene.
"I think I'm... his receipt."

Loki grinned, teeth sharp, eyes dancing.
"Well, tree-gift, welcome to the mess." He bowed,
mockingly regal.
"What shall I call you?"
She paused.

Then: "Aurelya."

He cocked an eyebrow.
"You just made that up."

"No. You just did."

Next up:
- Aurelya explores the realms and her powers.
- Odin refuses to admit she's, his doing.
- Loki brings her to her first "god party" (which goes sideways).
- She meets Tyras (divine love interest).
- And a mortal named Nyric stumbles into the wrong realm at exactly the wrong time.

Chapter Two: Of Tree Sap, Fish Forms, and God Parties Gone Wrong

[Scene: The Realm of Midgard – A Forest Edge, Dawn light]

Aurelya sat barefoot in the moss, crown catching the sun like it had stolen daylight. Her lion, a golden giant with knowing eyes, lay beside her, tail swishing. The dragon curled lazily in the branches overhead, scales glinting deep emerald and ember.

Aurelya frowned at the object in her hand.

"What… is this?"
Loki, now fully in fish form (a salmon, naturally), flopped near a shallow creek and somehow still managed to look smug.

"It's a spoon."
"No, it isn't. It's wooden and flat."
"Which makes it… a spoon."

She stared.

"You brought me a cursed salad stick from Alfheim because you think it's enchanted?"

"Not enchanted, bewitched. There's a difference," Loki said, transforming in a flash back to himself, now perched upside down in a tree like a particularly dramatic bat.
"Also, I stole it."

She sighed and handed it back.

"You're going to get us banned from another realm."

"Us?" Loki laughed. "Darling, you were born from a tree. You're already on most watchlists."

[Flashback: Asgard – 3 Days Ago – The Party That Went Wrong]

The party was… glowing. Literally. Floating lanterns, golden goblets, far too much divine ego packed into one shimmering hall. Gods postured, Valkyries danced, and Tyras, the tall, silent storm of divine law, watched from the shadows.
Aurelya walked in, radiant and unfamiliar. Half the room whispered. Odin choked on his mead. Loki made finger guns at her.

"Everyone, this is Aurelya," he declared. "She's technically your cousin or your sapling or your divine tax write-off, unclear, but do be nice."

Odin gulped. Frigg raised an eyebrow.

Then Tyras stepped forward.
Aurelya's eyes met his like thunderclouds meeting wildfire.

"You're not supposed to exist," he said.

"Neither are half the things Loki's turned into," she replied sweetly.

Someone snorted mead out their nose.

[Back to Present – Forest Edge]

"So Tyras is mad because I'm not listed in the divine family tree?" Aurelya asked.
Loki flicked the fake spoon.

"He's mad because you make him feel things he can't rule over."

“That sounds like a him problem.”

“Exactly why I like you.”

[Scene: Far off, between realms – A Rift Cracks]

Nyric stumbled through bramble and wind. The mortal scholar had been tracking an ancient energy surge from Midgard, but this was not Midgard.

The sky pulsed with light. A lion’s roar echoed.

And then… a girl with wings he could swear he’d seen in a dream stared at him like he’d just broken something important.

“Who are you?” she asked, crown glowing faintly.
He swallowed.
“I… I don’t know how I got here. But I think I’m supposed to help.”

Chapter Three: The Dragon Debt and the Dwarven Disaster

Starring: Loki, an auction gone wrong, Tyras with a sword, Nyric on his first quest, and a very angry dragon.

[Scene: Nidavellir – The Dwarven Halls]

"Let me get this straight," Aurelya said, blinking slowly.
"You sold my dragon."

Loki adjusted his cuffs, avoiding her gaze.
"I wouldn't say sold… More like… temporarily rehomed in exchange for an enchanted ale barrel and a mood ring."

The dragon growled from inside a glowing cage forged of runes and something suspiciously called "sky-iron."

Aurelya's voice was calm, terrifyingly calm.
"A mood ring."
Loki grinned.
"It changes colour, Aurelya. It's incredible."

The dwarves, meanwhile, were ecstatic.
"Best deal of the century!" shouted one, holding the ring aloft.
"This one shifts between wrath and disapproval!"
Aurelya cracked her knuckles. Her lion leaned in with a low rumble. The dwarves backed up a step. Loki took two.

[Suddenly – Divine Reinforcements Arrive]

A silvery gust swept through the hall.

Tyras appeared in a swirl of ice and command, cloak billowing like he had very strong opinions about justice.

"Loki."
His voice had the weight of law.

Loki raised a hand. "Before you get angry"
"You sold a celestial dragon to metal-bearded gremlins." Tyras snapped.
"Drunken metal-bearded gremlins," Aurelya corrected.
One dwarf burped a glittery hiccup in agreement.
Tyras drew his blade. Lightning licked the edges.

"Undo it. Now."

[Outside – As Chaos Ensues Inside]
Nyric paced. He didn't want to intrude, but also…
the roar echoing from inside was probably the
dragon, and possibly Aurelya in "mildly furious
goddess" mode.

He felt wildly out of place.

Then the lion approached.
Stared at him.
Sat down beside him.

Nyric blinked.

"Do I, uh, say hello?" he asked awkwardly.

The lion nudged his hand gently.

And then… purred.

[Back Inside – Dragon vs. Contract]

"According to dwarven law," one of them began,
holding a tiny scroll, "the transaction is binding
unless"

Aurelya stepped forward, eyes glowing starlight.

She reached into her crown, pulled a shard of Yggdrasil sap, pure essence, and held it up.

All the dwarves gasped.

"Yggdrasil relic. Nullifies all deals made in its presence," she said smoothly.

The dragon's cage snapped open.

It strutted out like it had allowed itself to be sold for the drama.

It licked Loki once, burning his boot, and curled up beside Aurelya with a loud huff.

Tyras sheathed his sword.
"That could've gone worse."

Loki grinned, singed.
"That could've gone a lot worse."

[Later – Outside the Halls, By the River]
Nyric sat by the fire, turning a map over in his hands.

Aurelya joined him, handing him a roll of dried fruit and bread.

"Thanks," he mumbled.
Then, hesitantly:
"Why did you let me come with you?"

She shrugged.
"Lion likes you."

Nyric smiled nervously.

"Also," she added, "there's something in your fate that pulled you into this. The tree doesn't mess around."

He looked at her, stars reflecting in her eyes.

Then: "Where are we headed next?"

She smiled.

"To the realm where nothing dies. Because that's where the sword was last seen."

Interlude: Origins & Secrets

Where memories stir, oaths break, and fates begin to unravel.

[Scene 1: Aurelya's First Memory – Within the Tree]

Before light, before voice, before names, there was pulse.

She remembered warmth.

Not heat like fire, but something older. Like sap thick with story.

Aurelya floated in golden amber, her form not yet fully formed. Roots whispered above her, voices of realms wrapping around her being like lullabies sung by stars.

Then …

A crack.

Her first sound: a grunt, followed by "OW BY THE RUNES WHO PUT A KNOT HERE?!"

Loki.

His foot had gotten stuck in the root bark.

She opened her eyes just in time to see him

upside-down, cursing at a squirrel.
It was her first memory of the world. And
somehow… it made her feel safe
[Scene 2: The Lion Speaks (Once)]

It was during a thunderstorm in Alfheim. Aurelya
sat beside her lion, wet cloak over both of them.

She whispered, "Do you ever get tired of
protecting me?"

The lion turned.

In a voice deep as mountain thunder, he said:
"Never."
And never spoke again.

Not because he couldn't.

But because one word was enough.

[Scene 3: Tyras's Oath]

Tyras knelt before the Aesir high court.

His hand on his own heart.
His sword point-down in the ice.

"I swear by the Bifrost, and the Nine Realms love

shall never sway my judgment. Emotion shall not cloud my will."

He had loved once. Long ago.
It ended in betrayal and war.

So now he served law.
Unshakable.
Until a girl born of tree sap looked at him like he mattered, not as a god, but as a man.
[Scene 4: Nyric's Dream]

He stands in a library that burns, yet nothing is consumed.
Books scream. The sky is stitched with runes he cannot read.

In the centre: a mirror.

He walks toward it
His reflection has no eyes.
Only a glowing sigil in the centre of his forehead.

It pulses like the tree.
A woman in the mirror whispers:

"You were marked before birth. She is your balance. But you are... her undoing."

He wakes, gasping.

Aurelya is already looking at him.

"I felt that" she says.

[Closing Scene – Campfire That Night]
Loki roasts stolen mushrooms. The dragon
snores. The lion watches stars.

Tyras sits far from the fire.

Nyric asks, quietly:
"Do you think we're all just playing out what the
tree already decided?"

Aurelya answers:
"Maybe. But the tree never had to deal with
Loki."
He raises his mushroom skewer like a toast.
"You're welcome."

Everyone laughs except Tyras, who almost
smiles.
And somewhere, deep in the roots of the
universe, the sword pulses. Waiting.

Next in Chapter Four:

The Realm of Eternal Stillness, where time stops, shadows whisper, and the sword's trail begins.

Chapter Four: The Realm of Eternal Stillness

Where time is a prisoner, the past walks beside you, and the sword's silence screams.

[Scene: Entry to the Realm Crossing the Threshold]

The gateway to the Realm of Eternal Stillness wasn't a door.

It was a pause in the forest.
A moment that didn't end.
One step forward and time forgot to move.

Aurelya led the way, her crown dimmed as if even its light knew to quiet itself.
The lion hesitated. The dragon growled, low in its throat.
Loki muttered, "This place gives me the heebie-hálfar."

Tyras gripped his sword.
Nyric reached for Aurelya's hand and for a moment, she let him.

Then everything stopped.
[Scene: The Realm Itself]

They walked into a land frozen in mid-motion.

Waves curved upward but never crashed.
Leaves fell and hovered midair.
A deer stood mid-step across a creek, unmoving,
eyes wide alive but paused.

"What is this place?" Nyric whispered.

"It's where the gods bury time," Aurelya
answered.
"Where consequences were never allowed to
finish."

At the centre of the realm stood a tree not
Yggdrasil, but a mirror-echo of it.
Black bark. Silver leaves.
And in its roots… a gleam of blue.

The sword.

[Scene: The Sword of Threads – Just Out of
Reach]

It pulsed with sapphire light woven into the tree,

its hilt wrapped in vines of memory.
Aurelya stepped forward.

The realm resisted.
The roots whispered in languages only she and
the dragon understood.
She stopped.

"It's locked in place," she said. "Time won't let it
go."

Loki tried tossing a rock at it.
The rock hovered midair, eternally one inch from
the sword.
"Helpful," Tyras deadpanned.

"Oh come on, you loved it," Loki grinned.
[Scene: Nyric's Curse Awakens]

Nyric's eyes began to glow. Faint, but undeniable.

He reached toward the tree and the sword
twitched.

Not physically.

In time.

It skipped forward a second. Then again.

Aurelya's eyes widened.

"He's a key," she breathed.
"To what, exactly?" Tyras asked, suddenly moving in front of her.

Nyric fell to one knee, head pounding.

Visions of the burning library. The sigil. The voice.

Then, his hand brushed the bark.

[Scene: Time Breaks]
The entire realm shuddered.

The deer fled. The waves crashed.

The stillness ended.

But the realm screamed as it died. A massive entity Warden of Time, formless and ancient emerged from the roots.
It roared, not in sound, but in undoing.

Reality frayed.
The dragon leapt. The lion shielded Aurelya.

Tyras drew his blade and stood between Nyric and the Warden.

"Get the sword!" Aurelya shouted.
Loki blinked.
"Wait me?"

"NOW!"

[Scene: The Sword is Taken]

Loki dashed.
Grabbed it mid-leap.
Time tried to erase him

But Aurelya's wings burst from her back, glowing with realm light.
She caught him, soared upward, slicing through the fraying magic with radiant force.
Tyras fought like the oath breaker he swore never to become.

Nyric stared at his hands as the sigil on his forehead pulsed like a heartbeat.

And the Warden screamed... then vanished.

Silence fell.
[Scene: Aftermath – Edge of the Realm]

They exited together, battered, quiet.

Aurelya held the sword. It hummed against her skin like it knew her.

Nyric leaned against a tree, eyes shut.

Loki sat on a rock, panting.
"No more still realms. Please. Ever."

Tyras looked at Aurelya.

"That boy is marked. If he loses control, he'll tear time apart."

Aurelya looked toward Nyric.

And said softly, "Then we don't let him lose."

END OF CHAPTER FOUR

Coming up:
Chapter Five: The Broken Oracle, the Lost Realm of Dreams, and a vision that shows Aurelya her end or her beginning.

Side Story Three: The Dragon's Hidden Name

Because true names carry power. And hers has not been spoken in millennia.
[Scene: A Moonlit Cliff – Realm of Whispering Stones]
The fire crackled low. Everyone else slept except Aurelya and the dragon.

It lay beside her, half-curled, scales glinting like molten starlight.

"You've never told me your name," Aurelya whispered.

The dragon opened one eye. A slow exhale warmed the stones beneath them.

"Because it's not safe," she said, voice deep and ancient.

Aurelya tilted her head. "You trust me to carry you across realms. But not your name?"

The dragon's gaze softened.
"I trust you too much to burden you with it."

[Flashback: When the Name Was Last Spoken]
Long ago, before gods danced across realms, the
dragon was born from the first flame that
touched Yggdrasil's lowest root.

She was given a name by the root itself a name so
powerful it echoed through all Nine Realms.

When spoken, it could summon fire from stars,
break illusions, or unlock sealed time.

One day, a god greedy for power spoke it aloud.

The dragon burned a kingdom to stop him.

Since then, she sealed the name away.

[Present – The Trust Moment]
Aurelya reached out, palm on the dragon's
forehead.

"I would never use your name against you."

The dragon blinked slowly.

Then whispered:
"Veyrath."

The stones around them glowed faintly. The fire

flared. The sword at Aurelya's hip hummed in recognition.

"It means...?"
"Breath of the Beginning."

[Twist]
From the shadows beyond the firelight, Nyric stirred.

He wasn't asleep.

And the name burned itself into his memory uninvited but destined.

Side Story Four: Nyric's Journal Entry

Entry #17
The goddess looked at me again today like I was… known. Not just seen. I should run. But the tree won't let me.

I feel the curse tightening. The dream from the Still Realm it's changing. She's in it now.

But she's not screaming.
She's laughing.

I don't know what that means.
Loki's Notes in the Margins (in green ink):
• "She is laughing. At your hair."
• "Next time, just ask her to braid it. It's a whole thing."
• "Also, if you do explode into shadow magic, warn us. Preferably before breakfast."

Up Next: Chapter Five – The Broken Oracle, the Realm of Dreams, and a vision that shows Aurelya her end or her beginning.

Chapter Five: The Broken Oracle & the Realm of Dreams

Where visions lie, truths bleed, and fates collide in starlit riddles.

[Scene: Realm of Dreams – Gate of Slumbering Light]
The entrance wasn't a gate in the traditional sense.

It was a breath.

A step into air that shimmered like sleep and smelled of forgotten lullabies.

As the group crossed the veil, their bodies remained on the forest floor outside the realm. Their minds souls entered Somvaldr, the Realm of Dreams.

Aurelya walked first.

Here, her wings never retracted. Her crown glowed with steady calm. But the air felt… wrong.

The dream realm was flickering.
"Something is unravelling," she murmured.
Loki appeared beside her, dressed suddenly in an oversized nightshirt with 'Don't Wake the Trickster' written in glittering runes.

"If a bed tries to seduce me again, I'm leaving."
[Scene: The Broken Oracle]
They found her in the heart of the realm: a floating figure of glass and shadow, cracked down the middle.

The Oracle of Somvaldr.

She opened eyes that wept ink.

"The sword has chosen but it bleeds its wielder."
Aurelya stepped forward.
"Show me."

The Oracle's hands cupped her face.

Visions spilled out like smoke,
[Vision: Aurelya's End… or beginning?]
She stood alone beneath the shattered World Tree. The Nine Realms fractured above her, stars falling like feathers. Nyric knelt before her, dark tendrils crawling up his arms.

Tyras stood behind him sword drawn, eyes wet with fury.

"You have to choose," said a voice.

Her own reflection stood beside her.

"One will break you. One will betray you. One will bury you."
[Back to Reality – All Dreamers Reeling]
Aurelya snapped back. The Oracle cracked further, groaning.

"The sword must pass through three hearts," she whispered. "One of love, one of shadow, one of truth."

The sword at Aurelya's side shimmered faintly.

Nyric gasped. A sigil appeared briefly on his chest.

Tyras was already watching her.

Loki, unusually quiet, leaned against a column of dream light.
"You always make things so dramatic," he whispered.
[Scene: Exit – Realms Colliding]

The realm shook. A shadow, not dream, not night, leaked in through the cracks.

"Something else has entered," Tyras said, eyes narrowing. "Something that doesn't sleep."

They fled through the veil.

The dragon roared.

The Oracle shattered behind them.

[Closing Scene – Outside the Realm, Real World Night]
Campfire flickering. Everyone silent.

Aurelya sat alone, sword in her lap, staring into the flames.

Nyric approached but didn't speak.
She looked up.

"Three hearts," she said. "And only one survives."

He looked away.
"Maybe we rewrite the prophecy."

She gave him a tired smile.

"We'll have to. Because I'm not letting either of you die for me."

From the trees, Tyras watched. And for the first time… considered breaking his vow.

Next Up:
Chapter Six: The War Before the War – God Council, Secret Betrayals, and Loki's "Oops I Started a Cult Again" Situation.

Chapter Six: The War Before the War

Featuring: A God Council with trust issues, a prophecy torn in half, and Loki's regrettable side hustle as a cult leader (again).

[Scene: Asgard – The Hall of Echoed Oaths]
The golden dome of the council hall shimmered with divine tension.

Aurelya sat at the far end of the table, flanked by Tyras and Loki (who was eating grapes he definitely hadn't brought).

Frigg sat in silence. Odin finally returned from his nine-day tree retreat with leaves in his beard and no sense of irony. Freya raised one perfectly sculpted eyebrow and muttered, "So the tree grew a girl now?"

"Technically," Loki chirped, "it grew a woman with better hair than most of you."

Odin frowned.
"And now the sword sings again. The realms shift. Dreams scream. Tell us why now?"

Aurelya stood, calm.
"Because the sword is waking up. And something's waking with it."

The council began bickering.

Then a Valkyrie burst through the doors.
"There's a… situation in Vanaheim," she said, hesitating.
"Apparently… Loki has a cult."

Loki choked on a grape.
[Scene: Vanaheim Loki's "Totally Chill and Harmless Worship Circle"]
Aurelya, Tyras, and Nyric stepped through the portal to find…

Dozens of flower-crowned followers chanting in a field. Wearing mismatched robes. Building a giant golden statue of Loki riding a goose.

Aurelya stared.
"Is that… a shrine made of turnips?"

Loki appeared, adjusting his ceremonial sash made of snakes.

"In my defence, I told them I was a gardening god."

Nyric blinked.
"How… did this happen?"

"I sneezed in the market, someone thought it was a blessing, next
thing I knew I was giving advice on carrot fertility."

Tyras: "We're leaving."
[Back at Camp – Tension Brews]
Later that night, Aurelya confronted Loki.

"You keep turning chaos into comedy. Why?"

He was quiet.

Then:
"Because if they laugh… they don't look too close.
They don't ask why a god of mischief can't sleep
without seeing fire."

She touched his shoulder gently.
"You're not alone anymore."

Loki looked at her. Smiled.
"Don't tell the cult."
[Scene: Council Again – Secrets Revealed]

Freya demanded the sword be destroyed. Odin said it was fate. Frigg just listened.

Tyras stood.
"The sword is already bonded. To her."
Aurelya stepped forward.
"We're not destroying anything. We're going to the realm it came from."
"The roots are shaking. But we're not running. We fight."

Everyone went quiet.
Then Frigg rose.
"You have one chance. Win back the roots. Or we burn the branch you came from."

Loki: "Wow, mum energy."

Coming up:
 Chapter Seven: Return to the First Flame –
Where the sword was forged, truths are tested, and Nyric's darkness finally speaks.

Chapter Seven: Return to the First Flame

Where the sword was born, the roots whisper secrets, and darkness demands to be seen.

[Scene: The Path to the Flame forge – Beneath All Realms]
The journey took them lower than Helheim.

Beneath even the roots of Yggdrasil, where stone became memory and heat was the only truth.

They walked through obsidian tunnels that glowed with ember veins, led by Aurelya's sword humming in rhythm with the fire below.

Loki lagged slightly behind.
"Anyone else feel like we're walking into someone's angry fireplace?"

Nyric didn't laugh. He'd been quiet for days. The sigil on his forehead had begun to glow even when he slept.

Tyras walked beside Aurelya, but not too close.
"You know," he said softly, "the last time anyone came down here… it forged a war."

Aurelya replied:
"Then maybe it's time someone forged a peace."
[Scene: The Flame forge – Birthplace of the
Sword]
The chamber was alive with flame.

Massive gears turned without source. Chains
dangled from nowhere. Lava flowed in spirals.

And in the centre: the Forge of Origins, an anvil
carved from a petrified star.

The sword in Aurelya's hand pulled toward it.

Whispers rose from the fire.

She was never meant to wield it.
It belongs to the three.
The binding is incomplete.

[Nyric Breaks]
He stumbled forward.

Fell to his knees.

Dark tendrils burst from the sigil on his chest
reaching toward
the sword.

Aurelya grabbed it, trying to pull away.

The forge flared.

Nyric screamed.

"It's mine! It called me before I was born! Don't you see it?"

Tyras moved to strike but Aurelya blocked him.

"No!" she shouted.
"He's not the enemy. The sword is waking what was buried inside him."

Loki stepped between the fire and Nyric.

"Alright, shadow boy, either pull yourself together or I'm giving your diary to the dwarves."
That did the trick.

Nyric collapsed, breathing hard. The tendrils retracted. The sigil dimmed.

[The Revelation]

Aurelya knelt before the forge and placed the sword upon the star-anvil.

A voice rose not flame, not forge, but root-deep.

"Three hearts. One path. One must fall. Or the realms will."

The sword glowed then split.
Not broken.
Revealed.

A hidden blade within the blade.

One for her.

One for… someone else.

She turned to Nyric and Tyras.
And for the first time, both blades hummed in response.

[Closing Scene – Edge of the Forge]
They camped in silence just outside the Flame forge's heat.

Aurelya held both blades in her lap.

Tyras sharpened his silence beside her.
Nyric slept restlessly, the dragon curled around him protectively.

Loki threw rocks into lava and made faces at the sparks.

Finally, Aurelya whispered:

"They said one must fall."

The lion lifted his head.

"Then find another way."

Next up:
 Chapter Eight: The Shadow Crown – A new enemy rises, wearing a face from Aurelya's past. And one of your team is not who they claim to be.

Chapter Eight: The Shadow Crown

Where illusions break, a familiar face returns twisted by darkness, and betrayal blooms beneath starlight.

[Scene: Realm of Fractured Skies – The Gathering Storm]
The sky above them cracked like glass.

Lightning danced across empty air, yet no thunder followed.

They had followed the trail of the sword's twin hums to a broken realm between realms once part of the Tree, now severed. Floating islands twisted midair, tethered by fading magic and the screams of dying stars.

Aurelya held the two blades. They hummed in unison... and then screeched as they approached the central island.

Loki whispered,
"That's either a terrible sign... or someone very stylish is nearby."

They stepped forward.

And found her.

[Scene: The Enemy Revealed – The Crowned
One]
A woman stood before them, cloaked in shadow
and wearing a twisted version of Aurelya's
crown.

Same eyes. Same wings.
But where Aurelya glowed this one devoured
light.

Nyric's breath caught.

Tyras stepped in front of Aurelya, hand on
sword.

The woman smiled.

"You left me behind."

Aurelya froze.

"I never… what?"

The woman took a step forward.
"When the Tree split. When it cast me into the

dark and kept you in the light. I am your shadow.
I am your other half. Your forgotten twin.”

[Flashback: The Sapling Split]
Long ago, during Odin's nine nights on the tree,
the sap gave two pulses of life.

One rose into Aurelya.
The other was cast downward, swallowed by the
void beneath the roots.

Formed in isolation.
Fed by broken dreams and realm runoff.
She became what the light feared: Veyna, the
Shadow Crown.

[Back to Present – The Confrontation]
“I don't want to kill you,” Aurelya said softly.

“You won't have to,” Veyna replied. “Because
someone already plans to.”

She snapped her fingers.
“Come forward, traitor.”

A figure stepped from behind the floating pillar.

It was one of their own. Cloaked. Hooded.

And when the face lifted

Tyras.

[Scene Twist: The Second Tyras]
Aurelya gasped.

The other Tyras, the one beside her, turned sharply. Sword drawn.

The new one smirked.

"How long did you think I could be bound by an oath I never made?"

Loki:
"Alright, we officially need name tags."

The Shadow-Tyras shimmered then morphed. It wasn't Tyras at all.

**It was a trickster spirit. A shifter known as Myrdyn, long exiled from Vanaheim. **

"I earned their trust for months," he hissed. "Slept beside your fire. Tasted your food. And now... I deliver your doom."

[Battle Begins – The Sky Splits]
Veyna raised her hand shadows leapt from the ground.
Myrdyn lunged at Aurelya.

But…

The real Tyras stepped in the way.

His sword met Myrdyn's with a sound like thunder forged.

The blades Aurelya's twin swords flew from her hands mid-fight and were caught

One by Aurelya. One by Nyric.

The sword accepted him.

The sigil on his forehead glowed so brightly it burned through his shirt.

Aurelya called out:

"Nyric are you with me?"

His eyes blazed.

"To the end."

[Closing Scene – Veyna's Warning]
The fight drove Veyna back, wounded but smiling.

"You delay the end," she whispered, fading into smoke.

"But the Tree remembers. And soon… the third heart will break."

Then she vanished.

Next Up:
Chapter Nine: The Mirror of Memory   Aurelya confronts the truth of her creation, Nyric's curse reveals its source, and Tyras makes an impossible choice.

Chapter Nine: The Mirror of Memory

Where the past breathes, the curse speaks, and the line between choice and fate finally begins to blur.

[Scene: The Withered Vale – Entrance to the Mirror Sanctum]
Aurelya stood before a gate made of woven bark and gold-veined stone.

It pulsed faintly, not in rhythm with the sword, but with her heartbeat.

Loki leaned close and whispered,
"You sure this isn't just a very fancy tree hugger's mausoleum?"
She didn't laugh.

Because this was it.

The last place Yggdrasil stored its truths.

Behind the gate: the Mirror of Memory capable of revealing any soul's entire truth, stripped of ego, illusion... even love.

Tyras touched her arm.
"You don't have to do this."

She looked at him, eyes glowing, mouth steady.

"I already did. When I was born."
[Scene: The Mirror – Aurelya's Reflection Breaks]
Inside the sanctum, the Mirror hung suspended in rootlike tendrils.

Its surface was silver but shimmered like a living sky.
When Aurelya stepped in front of it, her reflection blinked first.

Then smiled.

"You are not who you think you are," it said.

[Vision: The Hidden Creation]
The mirror showed her:

Not two saplings.
Three.
One rose into light Aurelya.
One fell into shadow Veyna.
And the third…

Was neither born nor lost.
It was stored.
A seed not yet grown.
A backup.
A balance.
A fail-safe.

Still pulsing at the centre of the Tree.
Waiting.

[Back to Present – Aurelya Reels]
She stumbled back.

"I wasn't meant to be a saviour…"

Nyric stepped forward.

"You were meant to be the warning."

The Mirror turned.

"And you," it said to Nyric, "were never cursed."
"What?"

[Nyric's Truth – The Curse Was a Lock]
The sigil on Nyric's body glowed bright blue.

The Mirror showed him a vision:

He was born from a mortal mother, but touched at birth by the Tree itself.
His mind fractured not from darkness, but from being given too much power too early.

The "curse" was a binding placed by the gods to stop his magic from consuming him.

He wasn't marked for death.
He was marked for containment.

A walking key not to open the sword, but to open Aurelya.

He wasn't her undoing.
He was her awakener.
[Scene: Tyras's Breaking Point]
Tyras had watched in silence.
Too much truth.
Too many unravelling threads.

"If she wasn't meant to wield the sword… if he was meant to unlock her… then what am I?"
Aurelya looked at him.

"You are my choice."
[Closing Scene – The Mirror's Final Prophecy]
The Mirror pulsed.

A new voice spoke, ancient and final.

"The Third Heart awakens soon. One of you must step into the roots and take its place. Or the Tree dies."

A silence heavier than prophecy followed.

Then Loki coughed.
"Just to clarify: does the 'step into the roots' part sound funeral-y to anyone else?"

Next Up:
 Chapter Ten: The Root Chamber – Three paths, one sacrifice, and a war no prophecy predicted.

Chapter Ten: The Root Chamber

Where time grows in knots, love is weighed against destiny, and someone must choose to disappear… so the worlds may remain.
[Scene: Beneath the Beneath – The Descent to the Root Chamber]
No paths led here.

They walked on memory.

Beneath lava, beneath ice, beneath the dreams of gods and the ashes of stars.

Roots, thick as towers, wound in impossible directions, some pulsing with light, some long decayed.
Aurelya felt each beat like a throb in her own chest.

The lion walked beside her.
The dragon above.
Nyric behind her, and Tyras ahead.
Loki? Loki was attempting to "casually whistle" while carving secret runes into his belt.

"What are you doing?" Tyras asked suspiciously.

"Insurance," Loki said. "Or a goodbye gift.
Depending on who dies."
No one laughed.
[Scene: The Root Chamber – A Living Heart]
They arrived.

The Root Chamber was not a room.
It was a womb.

A living hollow inside the base of Yggdrasil.
Golden sap ran in rivers.
Leaves floated midair.
And in the centre a pulse.

A half-formed being inside a cocoon of realm-
thread and bark.
The Third Heart.

Not born. Not awake.

Waiting for one of them to take its place.
To feed the Tree.
To keep the balance.
[The Choice]
The Mirror had spoken.

One of you must step in.
The Tree must remain three.
A light. A shadow. A seed.

Aurelya looked at Tyras.

He stepped forward.

"It should be me."

Nyric blocked him.
"No. I was made for this. I've always known I
wasn't meant to live a full life."

Aurelya shook her head, wings trembling.

"No. You're both wrong."

She stepped toward the cocoon.
[Twist – The Lion Intervenes]
Suddenly, the lion growled.

Louder than any sound before.

Then spoke.

"None of you must enter."

A hush fell.
"The Tree has always fed on sacrifice. It is time it
learns another way."

He stepped forward the oldest being in the

chamber.
Born before Aurelya.
Born with the Tree.

He was its first guardian.
And its most loyal.

Aurelya reached for him.

"Please don't"
He looked back.

"You are the future. Let the past rest."

And he stepped into the cocoon.

The roots shivered.
The Tree sighed.

The Third Heart pulsed complete.

[Scene: After the Sacrifice]
The cocoon closed.

The Root Chamber began to fade.
Outside, across all Nine Realms life stirred.

Frozen rivers melted.
Ashen fields bloomed.

Forgotten gods woke from slumber.

The Tree had been fed.

But not through blood.

Through devotion.

[Closing Scene – Campfire Again]
They sat quietly.

Tyras cleaned his blade.

Nyric stared into the sky.
Loki tried to summon a squirrel and failed.
(Don't ask.)

Aurelya held a leaf in her hand golden, and warm.
It had appeared where the lion once stood.

She smiled.

"We're not done."

Nyric looked at her.

"You mean the war?"

She nodded.

"I mean the real one."

Next up:
 Chapter Eleven: Veyna's Return, the Battle of the Branches, and the Rise of the Forgotten Gods.

Chapter Eleven: The Battle of the Branches

Where realms align for war, Aurelya faces her twin in open combat, and gods forgotten, forbidden, and fallen rise again.

[Scene: The Whispering Canopy Nine Realms Converge]

The skies shimmered with fault lines.

Branches of Yggdrasil, once unseen, snapped into view like a divine nervous system pulsing with intent.

The Nine Realms, held apart for eons, were now closer than ever. Too close.
"They're colliding," Tyras said, watching Alfheim and Muspelheim blink in and out beside Midgard.

"No," Aurelya said softly.
**"They're merging."

Loki adjusted his cloak.
"You know, when I said I wanted to feel more

connected to my heritage, this wasn't what I meant."

[Scene: Veyna Returns the Shadow Crown Commands]

From a floating branch above them, black sap dripped like blood.

Veyna stood upon it.
Crown sharpened.
Wings like raven smoke.
Eyes glowing with void-fire.

And behind her…

The Forgotten Gods.

Exiled beings cast out long ago for crimes like love, rebellion, or losing favour in some divine game.
They marched behind Veyna now led by fury, promised restoration.

"You saved the Tree," Veyna called to Aurelya.
"But forgot the roots still rot. I will not heal what betrayed me. I will replace it."

[The First Clash Blade vs. Mirror]

Aurelya rose into the air, twin blades burning in her hands.

Veyna rose to meet her, pulling her weapon a mirror edged in blacklight.

They clashed midair.

Memory and possibility sparked off their weapons, realities split and stitched again with every blow.

Loki, watching below, nudged Nyric.

"Ten gold leaves on Aurelya."

Nyric: "You have gold leaves?"

Loki: "Not yet, but I plan to steal them off a Valkyrie's cloak."

[Ground Battle Forgotten vs. Familiar]

Tyras led the defence, sword glowing, shield bearing the mark of oaths broken and reforged.

Nyric unleashed his power fully for the first time, shadow and light weaving through the air like celestial ink.

The dragon and lion's final gift, a gust of memory swept through the battlefield, reminding every realm why they once stood united.

Even the Forgotten hesitated.
Until Veyna screamed:
"They abandoned you! You owe them NOTHING!"

And the war resumed.

[Mid-Battle Revelation The Real Enemy]

As Aurelya and Veyna locked blades again, something shifted.

A crack appeared in the sky.

Not from their weapons.

From above.

A being of pure white stepped through.

Not light.

Not shadow.

But Blankness.
A forgotten force beyond even the Tree.

The one who had cast Veyna into darkness in the first place.

"You were never meant to exist," it said to both of them.
"Neither of you are real. You were grown… to delay destruction. Not prevent it."

[Closing Scene: The Alliance Forms]

Veyna faltered.

Aurelya lowered her blades.

"Then let's stop being delays," she said.

"Let's be the storm that rewrites the ending."

The twin sisters turned.

For the first time, side by side.

The Forgotten Gods hesitated.

Then followed.

Even the Blankness paused.

And recalculated.

Next Up: Chapter Twelve: The Library at the
Edge of All Things – Secrets of the Creators, and
the plan to rewrite fate itself.

Chapter Twelve: The Library at the Edge of All Things

Where the first stories are written, fate is inked in blood and bark, and the truth behind the Tree is revealed at last.

[Scene: The Final Realm Outside Time, Beyond Death]

The path appeared only when no one looked at it.

A backward-glancing trail of falling stars, lined with forgotten prayers and broken prophecies. Aurelya, Veyna, Tyras, Nyric, Loki, and what remained of their allied gods followed it in silence.

Ahead, carved into the space where light gave up:
The Library at the Edge of All Things.

Floating. Infinite. Built from petrified books, spiralling quills, and whispering leaves.
The front doors read:

"Here lies every version of what might be.

Do not knock unless you're prepared to undo what was."

[Scene: The Librarian Appears]

A figure with a head made of ink and a robe of paper turned to greet them.
The Librarian.

"I've been expecting you since before the Tree dreamed of itself."

Loki tilted his head.
"Why do you sound like you eat riddles for breakfast?"

The Librarian smirked.

"Because answers are dangerous on an empty stomach."

[Scene: The Books of Origin – The Truth Revealed]

The Librarian led them through rows of shifting storybooks with no titles, pages that changed depending on who held them.

He stopped before a pedestal.
On it: The Root Script, the original document. Not written in ink, but in living thread.

Aurelya approached.

The book opened itself.

And revealed:

There were never only nine realms.
There were ten.
One was hidden, The Realm of the Unwritten,
where fate is unformed, and time can be
changed.

It had been sealed off to keep "The Blankness"
out because it fed on possibility.

But now… it was bleeding through.

[The Decision]
The Librarian closed the book.

"There is one way to rewrite the script. But only
if you become part of it."

Aurelya frowned.
"You mean sacrifice?"

The Librarian shook his head.

"Worse. Authorship. If one of you writes the

ending, you can never be in it."
Everyone went silent.

Veyna looked at Aurelya.

"We were written into being. Maybe it's time we write back."

[Twist: Nyric Steps Forward]

"I'll do it."

Everyone turned.
Nyric stood with the Root Blade in one hand, and a page of the Living Script in the other.

"I was made to carry power too heavy for a mortal. Maybe that wasn't a mistake. Maybe it was a message."

Aurelya tried to speak, but he smiled.
"You made me feel real. That's enough."

[Scene: The Final Pen]
The Librarian handed him the Quill of Origin.

It pulsed like a heartbeat.

"Write well," he whispered.

Nyric stepped into the Unwritten Room.
And the door closed behind him.

[Closing Scene – A New Ending Begins]

The Library began to dissolve.

Reality rippled.
Aurelya fell to her knees tears in her eyes but peace in her heart.

Tyras lifted her gently.

Loki sat beside her.
"So… what happens now?"

She looked toward the horizon.
"Whatever he wrote."

And far above, in the canopy of stars

The Tree bloomed again.

Coming Next: Final Chapter: The Tenth Realm – The New World, Nyric's Legacy, and the Choice to Remember or Forget.

Final Chapter: The Tenth Realm

Where a new reality blooms, memory becomes a choice, and the last goodbye may not be the end.

[Scene: Awakening – Somewhere New, Yet Familiar]
Aurelya opened her eyes to birdsong.

Real birds.

The Tree stood tall, brighter than ever, its leaves tinged in soft gold, humming softly.

But the Nine Realms were different now.
Not separate. Not broken.
Braided together, flowing like rivers that had finally remembered they were part of the same sea.

And just above the roots...
The Tenth Realm.

A floating sanctuary of possibility never written, but now grown.
A place for dreams too wild for prophecy.

[Scene: The Cost]
They searched for Nyric.

He wasn't in the Tree.
Wasn't in the sky.
Wasn't in the wind.

He had written himself out of the story.

The script was finished, sealed into the bark of
the Tree itself, a single line glowing faintly:

Let them live in the world we never had to save.

Aurelya pressed her hand to the words.
Her tears shimmered like stars in sap.

Tyras stood beside her silently.

Loki placed a hand on her shoulder, soft for once.
"He chose us."

[Scene: The Choice]
The Librarian reappeared, faded and ghostlike
now.

"His final act was to offer a choice."
He opened one last page blank, save for a line:

You may forget. Live a life of peace. Never know pain, sacrifice, or me.

Or you may remember. Carry me. And shape what grows next.

Aurelya looked at her friends.

Tyras. Veyna. Loki. The dragon and lion's spirit pulsing in the wind.
She smiled.

"I choose to remember."

[Scene: Epilogue – The Tenth Realm Blooms]
Time passed.

Veyna became the new keeper of the balance between realms, guardian of what might have been.

Tyras taught oaths, but this time, how to break them when love demands it.

Loki… founded a floating comedy school. With questionable ethics. And an eel cult. (Yes, again.)

And Aurelya?

She became the Weaver of the Tenth Realm.

Spinning stories from light and shadow.
Writing new beginnings.
Planting dreams into the stars.

And every time she looked at the Tree
Saw that single glowing line

She whispered back:
"Thank you."

INTERLUDE: THE OTHER SIDE OF STILLNESS

While Aurelya rewrote fate…
Fraya was hiding behind a pillar, pretending not
to cry.

The Tree had plans for her, too.
They just weren't as polite.

Chapter Fourteen: Fraya Doesn't Cry Anymore

(Day One of Odin in the Tree)

Starring: Odin, Fraya (not Frigg, because this woman is her own mythology now), a suspicious goat, and the sound of a marriage unravelling louder than the World Serpent's sneezes.

It began with silence.
Not the sacred, spiritual kind Odin always claimed to seek but the marital kind. The kind that lasted twelve realms deep and echoed off kitchen walls for years.

Fraya stood at the base of Yggdrasil in her house robe silk, dramatic, with a coffee stain shaped like Asgard watching her husband tie himself to a tree again.

"Really?" she muttered. "Again, with the rope?"

Odin, perched solemnly halfway up the trunk, raised a hand in grand theatrical flair. "I must hang for nine days and nine nights to receive the runes of wisdom."

Fraya rolled her eyes. "Or you could just go to

couples' therapy. Like a normal immortal."
He ignored her. "This sacrifice is sacred"

"No, this marriage was supposed to be sacred,"
she snapped. "And yet here we are. You've got
ravens. I've got a rotisserie chicken and no one to
eat it with."

A suspicious goat wandered past and looked up
at Odin like even it thought this was a bit much.

Fraya had had enough. Centuries of "The World
Needs Me More Than You," of whispered secrets
and cryptic visions, of watching him suffer
publicly for attention while she raised gods and
monsters and empires with no thanks.

She climbed the first root of Yggdrasil, not to join
him, but to get a better view of the life she was
leaving behind.

"You think this tree is a sacrifice?" she called up.
"I sacrificed me. My dreams. My peace. For your
prophecy."

Odin blinked. "Fraya"

But she wasn't done. Her voice was steady now.
Cold. The kind of calm only a woman on the edge

of her own freedom could hold.

"You want nine days of wisdom, Odin?
Try spending one day truly hearing me.
But you never could. So, I'm done whispering
beneath your thunder."
She reached into her robe, pulled out a scroll
titled "Divorce Rune (Draft 7)", and tied it to the
tree just under his feet. A gentle reminder that
some ropes are chosen and some are broken.
Somewhere in the Nine Realms, thunder cracked.
It wasn't Odin.

Chapter Fifteen: Day Two – The Goat Union Pickets Yggdrasil

Starring: Odin (still tied to a tree), Fraya (glowing up), The Goat Guild of Midgard (GGM), and Loki with a clipboard he may or may not have stolen.

Odin had barely finished mumbling his second mystical mantra when he was interrupted by... chanting.

Not ancient whispers. Not celestial voices.

No.
Goats.
A LOT of goats.
Holding picket signs.

"TREE IS NOT A TOILET."
"WE DEMAND A GRAZING CONTRACT."
"ODIN HANGS, GOATS PAY THE PRICE."

At the front stood a particularly well-groomed goat in a leather vest, dark sunglasses, and a clipboard. Her name was Helga. She was not here

for divine nonsense.
"Excuse me," she bleated, voice firm with union authority, "but this tree is now a certified Goat Sanctuary and the emotional support structure of seven endangered moss species."

Odin blinked. "I what?"

Helga didn't pause. "You have violated the GGM Treaty of 4E47B by turning this sacred habitat into a theatrical noose-themed pity party."
She turned. "BRING THE RUNE BANNERS, BOYS."

Goats poured out of bushes, waving ribbons that read:

"Yggdrasil Belongs to the Herd"
"You Can't Milk Enlightenment"
"Sacrifice is a Choice, Not a Lifestyle"

Loki emerged from the side of the hill, munching on an oat bar and wearing a fake press badge.

"Hey Odin, thoughts on being cancelled by goats? Asking for the Nine Realms."

Odin groaned and muttered something about destiny.

Helga wasn't finished. She stepped closer.
"We goats are sick of divine egos. Do you know how many druid weddings we've had to cancel because you're 'vibrating between realms' right where the cake goes?"

From somewhere below the branches, a goat in a beret shouted:

"AND MY UNCLE SLIPPED ON A WISDOM DROPLET!"

Meanwhile, back in Asgard, Fraya was sipping mead in a silk robe, getting her nails painted by a Valkyrie named Hilda while reading "How to Emotionally Detach from Divine Man-Children."

"Did he reach enlightenment yet?" Hilda asked.

Fraya smirked. "No. But apparently the goats did."
And so, Day Two ended not with divine wisdom… but with Odin tied to a tree, being heckled by livestock, while somewhere in Midgard, a Viking poet wrote the very first protest song.

Chapter Sixteen: Day Three – Loki Tries to Sell the Tree to Dwarves for Beer Money

Starring: Odin (still in the tree), Loki (armed with charm and forged documents), suspicious dwarves, a squirrel who's seen too much, and a pop-up tavern with questionable licensing.

Odin was beginning to hallucinate.

By dawn of Day Three, he had started to confuse his left foot for the moon and was reciting riddles that no one asked for. Meanwhile, Yggdrasil was busy hosting an entirely different drama at its roots.

Loki had arrived.
Not with help. Not with wisdom.
But with a folding table, a fake deed to the tree, and an enchanted quill named Susan.

"Welcome, gentlemen!" Loki beamed, gesturing to two highly skeptical dwarves with pickaxes and trust issues. "Today only one-time offer the World Tree, slightly used, ancient, vibrationally powerful, and guaranteed to attract ravens!"

The dwarves stared.

"Isn't that Odin up there?" one asked.

"Pfft. Decorative. Adds value," Loki replied smoothly. "You could turn him into a feature. Hang your tools on him. Use him for brand awareness. Call it Odin's Oak Brewery!"

"Hmm…" muttered the other dwarf, inspecting the bark. "Bit too weepy for a tavern. Smells like regret and unresolved trauma."

Loki smiled wider. "Which is EXACTLY what your customers will relate to!"

Just as he unrolled the Forgery of Divine Ownership Scroll (complete with a doodle of Thor drinking from a sap bucket), a squirrel poked its head from a branch.

Ratatoskr. The gossip courier of the realms. And also the worst snitch this side of Helheim. "ODIN'S NOT DEAD, YOU LITTLE GRIFT GREMLIN," he screeched. "I HEARD HIM COMPLAINING ABOUT HIS HIP AN HOUR AGO."

Loki sighed. "Why do you always ruin my fun, you squeaky panic almond?"

Back in the tree, Odin stirred.

"Loki… are you selling my sacred trial of wisdom for mead money?"

Loki looked up, casually leaning on his table. "Would you rather I monetize your trauma or emotionally validate you? Because one of those pays."

The dwarves left unimpressed. The sale was off. But Loki, ever the opportunist, turned the table into a taco stand by midafternoon and made five gold coins from selling "Yggdrasil Bark Nachos."

Meanwhile, Fraya?
She launched her online coaching empire:
"Untangle Your Inner Roots: A Self-Love Journey for Goddesses with Shitty Husbands."

Business was booming.
And thus ended Day Three: with Odin questioning his divine authority, a squirrel writing a tell-all memoir, and Loki inventing side hustles faster than anyone could legally shut them down.
Onward to Day Four

NEXT: Fraya's going on a speed date… and she's bringing a Valkyrie as backup.

Buckle up, divine hearts, it's time for some goddess-level glow-up.

Chapter Seventeen: Day Four – Fraya Goes Speed Dating (with a Valkyrie Chaperone)

Starring: Fraya (finally thriving), Hilda the Valkyrie (wing woman and wine assassin), Thor's unsolicited opinions, and a surprise appearance by a very nervous demigod who brings a chicken.

Back in Asgard, while Odin mumbled "I am the tree, the tree is me…" to passing butterflies, Fraya was doing something radical:

 Having fun.
Wearing heels that made her feel like vengeance.
Drinking rosé with sparkles in it.
And tonight? Speed dating.

Yes, Fraya, once the First Lady of the Nine Realms, Goddess of Wisdom-by-Association, and unofficial co-signer of All Odin's Bullsh*t, was about to flirt. In public. With mortals and immortals. For her.

She arrived at the Valkyrie-hosted event in a velvet gown that screamed "I'm emotionally

unavailable, but in a really hot way."
By her side?
Hilda, the 6'5" battle-maiden of winged eyeliner
and judgment.

"No dwarves," Hilda said, scanning the room.
"They smell like mining and daddy issues."
"And no elves," Fraya added. "Too pretty. Makes
me nervous."

The first candidate approached.

Bachelor #1: Fenrir's Personal Trainer
Arms like thunder. Vocabulary like a wet sponge.
"So, like, are you into chains or what?"
Rejected.

Bachelor #2: Demigod Accountant
Brought a chicken for some reason. Sweated
profusely.
Cried when Fraya complimented his tunic.
"My ex never said nice things."
"That's because your ex was probably a raccoon
in a cloak," Hilda whispered.
Rejected (but chicken kept).

Bachelor #3: A Literal Fire
Not a god. Not a man. Just a flaming pile of divine
ego.

"I can warm your cold, goddess heart."
"I can call the fire department," Fraya
deadpanned.
Rejected with a bucket of wine.

By table seven, Fraya wasn't even pretending to
smile anymore. She sipped her wine, leaned
toward Hilda, and whispered:
"Do you think I'm broken?"
"No," Hilda said. "I think you've just spent so long
being quite next to Odin that you forgot your
voice makes thunderstorms jealous."
Fraya blinked. Then she laughed.
Across the room, Thor watched, deeply
uncomfortable.
"Should we... stop her?" he asked.
"She's speed dating, not summoning demons,"
Heimdall replied. "Let her have one night."

Back under Yggdrasil, Odin sneezed and
accidentally untied one arm.
"Fraya?" he called weakly. "I think I had a
vision... of your ankle?"
Ratatoskr threw a pinecone at his head.
Day Four ended with Fraya dancing barefoot
under starlight, Hilda cheering her on, and one
very flustered bartender asking, "Was that the
Fraya?"
Yes. Yes, it was.

Day Five Next: It's time for Thor to try therapy...
and promptly hit the therapist's couch with his
hammer.

Chapter Eighteen: Day Five – Thor Tries Therapy, Hits Couch with Hammer

Starring: Thor (emotionally constipated), a licensed Midgardian therapist named Susan, a very brave clipboard, and Odin still tied to a tree trying to telepathically scream "I'm the main character!"

It began as an intervention.

After Fraya's glow-up and Loki's taco stand nearly setting fire to the world tree, the Realms needed balance. Odin was still dangling from Yggdrasil muttering about "sacred roots" and "his shoulder cramp being metaphorical," and Thor?

Thor was… yelling at the sky again.
"WHY WON'T MY AXE LOVE ME LIKE MJÖLNIR DID?!"

So Fraya booked him a therapy appointment. On Midgard.
With Susan, who had three degrees, a lava lamp, and absolutely no idea who Thor was.

Scene: The Therapist's Office
Location: Midgard, Earth. Scented candles. A
single goldfish named Alan. And one very
uncomfortable god of thunder.

Susan smiled kindly. "So, Thor. Why are you here
today?"
"MY FAMILY IS FALLING APART.
MY FATHER IS IN A TREE.
MY MOTHER'S ON A SELF-LOVE JOURNEY.
MY BROTHER IS SELLING BURNT NACHOS.
AND MY HAMMER LEFT ME FOR A STORM GOD
IN ANOTHER REALM."

Susan blinked. "Okay. And how does that make
you feel?"

Thor narrowed his eyes. "STRONG."

Susan scribbled something that looked
suspiciously like "delusional with dimples."

"Do you ever feel… out of control? Like maybe
you hit things instead of dealing with emotion?"
Thor snorted. "Nonsense. I only hit couches. And
doors. And my feelings. With lightning."
Susan took a deep breath. "Let's try something
different. Pretend this pillow is your childhood
disappointment."

Thor stared. The pillow had a floral pattern.

Then, WHAM!
The pillow disintegrated under Mjölnir's
replacement axe, which was definitely not
licensed for use indoors.

"I HAVE CONFRONTED MY PAST!" Thor declared
triumphantly.
"AND SMOTE IT."

Susan looked at the shattered couch. Then at
Thor.
Then gently offered him a juice box.

"That was… a start."
Meanwhile, in Asgard, Fraya updated her blog:
 "Healing Is Not Linear Especially When Your
Brother Punches His Trauma."
Back under Yggdrasil, Odin sighed deeply.
"Perhaps Thor too seeks wisdom…"
Ratatoskr: "Your son thinks emotional regulation
is a combat sport."
Day Five ended with Thor being politely banned
from Earth therapy, Susan needing hazard pay,
and the goldfish Alan now believing in Norse
gods after witnessing an emotional lightning
storm.

Shall we ride into Day Six?
Odin hears a squirrel whisper the truth and
finally begins to unravel.

Chapter Nineteen: Day Six – The Squirrel Tells Odin He's the Problem

Starring: Odin (delusional and dangling), Ratatoskr (truth-teller with zero filter), Yggdrasil (tired of everyone's drama), and a guest appearance from an emotional support mushroom.

By Day Six, Yggdrasil had grown visibly annoyed.

Its leaves drooped like exhausted parents at a school play, its branches groaned every time Odin mumbled, and its roots had started pulling away from him like:

"Ugh… not this dude again."

Odin, for his part, was still hanging there stubborn, dramatic, and trying to enter a meditative state through sheer narcissism.

"I surrender myself… I sacrifice for all… I am the light"

"You're the problem, actually."

Odin's eyes snapped open.

Perched on a branch beside his head, balancing a tiny acorn like it was a microphone, sat Ratatoskr, the Realm's most chaotic gossip courier.
"I've spoken to literally everyone," the squirrel continued. "Fraya? Thriving. Thor? Screaming into a juice box. Loki? Selling edible runes. You? Dangling here thinking this is helping anyone."

"I'm seeking wisdom," Odin said defensively.

"No, you're avoiding your wife," Ratatoskr replied. "And being a tree ornament of self-pity isn't spiritual. It's sad."

Odin bristled. "You dare question my divine quest?!"

"Your 'divine quest' is an unpaid drama internship."

Yggdrasil shook slightly in what could only be interpreted as squirrel-approved applause.

Ratatoskr kept going.

"You didn't listen to your wife. You didn't listen

to your kids. You didn't listen to your kingdom.
Now the goats have a union, the gods are
emotionally unstable, and Fraya's writing an
eBook."

Odin began to protest, but Ratatoskr raised a tiny
paw.
"Do you even know why Fraya left?"
"She… grew weary of my… burden?"
"She grew weary of you treating her like your
emotional sidekick. She got tired of being the
footnote to your prophecy."

Silence.

For the first time in six days, Odin wasn't
narrating his own suffering.

He just… blinked.

"I miss her."

"Then climb down," the squirrel said simply. "Not
just from the tree but from your throne made of
ego."

He dropped a tiny emotional support mushroom
into Odin's lap and vanished into the canopy like
the mystical therapist he truly was.

Meanwhile, in Asgard…

Fraya added a new quote to her coaching altar:

"You can't heal a man who worships his wounds."

And in the distance, for the first time in ages…

Odin wept.

Day Six ended not with thunder, but with truth: small, sharp, and delivered by a rodent with better boundaries than most gods.

UP NEXT Day Seven

Fraya finally launches her own sub-realm within the 10th Realm and baby, it's divine.

Chapter Twenty: Day Seven – Fraya Launches Her Own Realm (And Doesn't Invite Odin)

Starring: Fraya (CEO of her own joy), Hilda (now her Realm Manager), a divine DJ named Beatdrasil, and one lonely raven trying to RSVP on Odin's behalf.

The Tenth Realm had many paths. Aurelya wove them. But some were stitched by others. Like Fraya, whose thread refused to be silent any longer.
By Day Seven, Fraya had stopped looking over her shoulder.

Gone were the days of "Maybe he'll change" and "Maybe if I just love harder."
She'd given the Nine Realms her best… and now? She was taking her tenth.

She called it: VYRA
(A realm for goddesses, mortals, and magical beings with good boundaries and expensive taste.)

It was warm, sunlit, scented with self-respect
and lavender, and built entirely on the principles
Odin had never mastered:

Radical joy
Emotional accountability
And perfectly symmetrical mood lighting
At the heart of the realm stood The Temple of
Reclamation, where Fraya greeted her first
visitors, survivors of toxic kings, overlooked
wives of fate, and one Minotaur who just needed
a place to cry.

"Welcome," she said, her voice lined with
thunder and silk.
"This is not a kingdom. It's a beginning."
Meanwhile... back in the Nine Realms...
Loki threw a Vyra Launch Party in his tavern
taco stand (now rebranded as "Tacos &
Trauma™").
He wore a "Team Fraya" shirt and sold Realm
Breakup Kits (contents: one scroll, one sass, and
one emergency confidence potion).

Thor showed up, confused, holding a houseplant.

"Is this a wedding?"
"No," said Hilda. "It's a coronation of self-worth."

"Do I still give her the plant?"
"Yes, sweetie."
Meanwhile, Odin sat beneath Yggdrasil, clutching his emotional support mushroom like it might apologise for everything.

A single raven returned from Vyra carrying a scroll.
It read:

"You're not unworthy.
You're just no longer my responsibility."
He stared at it. And for the first time, truly read it.
Back in Vyra, Fraya danced barefoot on marble warmed by sunlight and her own rebirth.

She didn't look back.

She didn't need to.
Day Seven ended not with an ending, but with a beginning and the quiet, glorious sound of a goddess choosing herself.
The final day, Day Eight
Odin finally understands everything…
But Fraya's already gone…

Chapter Twenty-one: Day Eight – Odin Finally Gets It (But She's Already Gone)

Starring: Odin (too late), Fraya (unreachable, not because she's cruel, but because she's healing), a fading thread of fate, and the last letter that never got sent.

The sky didn't thunder.
The tree didn't shake.
No ravens cawed.

On Day Eight, something far more terrifying happened to Odin:
He finally understood.

Not through pain.
Not through visions.
But in the stillness, the kind that comes after you've burned all your excuses.

He sat beneath Yggdrasil now, untied, unsummoned, no longer holy in his suffering, just a man who had mistaken silence for strength and distance for divinity.

He clutched the scroll Fraya had sent.
Not a spell. Not a plea.
"You're not unworthy.
You're just no longer my responsibility."

He read it a hundred times.
Each time, a little more of his armour cracked.

Because the truth was:
He thought if he suffered enough, he wouldn't
have to change.
He thought if he became wise enough, she'd wait.

But Fraya… Fraya had rewritten the myth.
She had stepped off the pedestal and walked into
her own sun.
He tried once to reach her.

He gathered old runes, whispered old names,
summoned ravens.
But they came back empty.

Fraya had left no forwarding realm.
Far away in Vyra, Fraya stood in a garden of
golden blossoms and unspoken victories.
Hilda approached her, gently.

"He's not coming, is he?"
"No," Fraya said softly. "And I'm not waiting."

She opened a small, worn letter the one she
never sent.
"Dear Odin,
I begged you to hear me.
I whispered my needs between your prophecies,
hoping you'd notice.
But you were always chasing stars,
while I drowned quietly on Earth.
So now I rise.
And I rise without you.
This is not the end of us.
It's the beginning of me."

She let the letter go.
The wind took it.
So did the pain.
Day Eight ended not with regret,
but with release.
And the story of a god who finally opened his
eyes,
only to find the love he'd taken for granted
had already flown...

Side Adventure One: Loki's Accidental Wedding to a Sea Witch

Starring: Loki (somehow both victim and cause), Aurelya (your celestial winged heroine), a sea witch with commitment issues, and Nyric showing up late with snacks.

It began, as many Loki stories do, with a dare, a disguise, and a suspicious conch shell.

"I just needed one hair from a kraken to finish the illusion spell," Loki explained.

"So naturally," Aurelya replied, folding her celestial wings with great restraint, "you told the Sea Witch Queen you wanted to marry her?"

"I panicked!" he cried. "She called me 'shiny' and made me soup!"

They stood in a coral palace made entirely of passive aggression and salt. Behind them, Sea Witch Queen Vyrmala glared lovingly at Loki through a mirror made of eel teeth.

"Where is my husband-to-be?" she purred across the psychic coral intercom.

"You told her you were a prince," Aurelya deadpanned.
"Technically not a lie," Loki shrugged. "I just didn't specify of what."
Enter Nyric, dripping seawater and holding a soggy box of cookies.

"Sorry, I'm late. I got stuck in a whirlpool. Also, I think a jellyfish cursed me."

Aurelya: "We're crashing an underwater wedding."
Nyric: takes a bite "Cool. Are we blowing something up or emotionally resolving it?"
Meanwhile, in the Bridal Cavern of Regret...

Vyrmala had summoned her family an octopus uncle who played the organ, twin Mer-sisters who hated Loki on sight, and a barnacle priest who was 400 years old and only spoke in riddles.

"Do you take this liar, uh, lover to bind with you until the tides forget their names?"

Loki smiled tightly. "Could I... possibly speak to the bride alone?"

She took him aside.

"You don't love me," she said quietly.
"No," Loki admitted. "But I like your power. And your soup."
"And you like the chase. Not the commitment."

"You too?" he blinked.

They looked at each other. Then burst out laughing.
"Let's fake our wedding," Vyrmala grinned.
"Crash the afterparty. Steal everyone's secrets."

Loki held out his hand. "Queen, you had me at chaos pact."
By the time Aurelya and Nyric burst in with a rescue plan involving glowing pufferfish and a sonic boom spell, the fake wedding had become the underground event of the season.

"Loki! What is happening?!"
"Marriage is a performance art piece, darling."

Later that night, as they floated home on a spell-whale made of music, Loki curled up between his two best friends and sighed.

"She said I was shiny," he whispered.

"You are," Aurelya said. "In the way stars are shiny right before they go supernova."

"Thanks," he smiled. "I think."

The Sea Witch sent him soup once a year after that. He never forgot her.

But he never got legally married again.

Too much paperwork.

Side Adventure Two: Nyric's Lost Journal from the Realm of Eternal Deadlines

Starring: Nyric (tired), a realm that runs entirely on bureaucracy and caffeine, and sentient paperwork that bites.

Entry One: DO NOT ENTER THIS REALM UNLESS YOU HATE JOY.

I don't know who approved this mission. It might have been me. I was running on three hours of sleep and half a prophecy.

This place The Realm of Eternal Deadlines is powered by dread and printer ink. Time doesn't pass here. It piles up.

Everything smells like burnt coffee and stale ambition.

The skies are grey.

The clouds spell "URGENT."

The birds deliver emails instead of songs. They cc your trauma.

Entry Two: I TRIED TO FIGHT A PRINTER. I LOST.

Found a temple made entirely of overdue tasks. There's a god here. His name is TPS. He wears a tie made of red tape. He speaks only in passive-aggressive memos.

He handed me a form titled: "APPLICATION TO REQUEST EMOTIONAL CLARITY (IN TRIPLICATE)."

I tried to fill it out, but the pen screamed when I touched it.

Entry Three: LOKI SENT ME A CARE PACKAGE. IT WAS JUST A NOTE THAT SAID "HAHA."

Aurelya managed to beam me a voice message through a fax machine. It said:
"You are not your productivity. You are stardust and sarcasm. Come home soon."
I cried into my keyboard. The keyboard filed a complaint.

Entry Four: I MET THE ORIGINAL GOD OF BURNOUT.

She looked like a star that gave up shining and took up knitting instead.
She whispered: "Child, if everything is urgent, then nothing is sacred. Go. Let the world miss one thing."
So, I did. I walked out mid-form.
Alarms screamed. Time tried to follow me.
But I whispered, "No." And the whole realm paused for just one second.

Final Entry: I'm back. And I brought cookies.

Aurelya tackled me into a hug.
Loki pretended he hadn't cried but his eyeliner was smudged.
The lion purred.
I left the Realm of Eternal Deadlines behind.
But I brought one page with me.
On it was written: "You are allowed to rest. You are allowed to exist beyond achievement."
I keep it in my cloak now. Right next to the snacks.
Next up: Aurelya's Surprise Visit to One of Loki's Other Families (and the chaos that unfolds when she plays polite guest... until the kids ask who she really is). Ready?

Side Adventure Three: Aurelya's Surprise Visit to One of Loki's Other Families

Starring: Aurelya (too polite for this), Loki (squirming), a dozen magical children with suspiciously shiny teeth, and one ex-wife with questions and a flaming rolling pin.

It started with a knock.
Not hers.

Aurelya opened the cottage door expecting a parcel of prophecy.
Instead, she found a child. With green eyes.
Mischievous grin.
"Hi! Are you my new stepmom?"

Aurelya blinked.

"...I'm sorry, what?"

Before she could finish the sentence, twelve more children spilled through a magical portal behind him like enchanted dominoes.
Each one looked vaguely like Loki.
One had horns.

One had antlers.
One just hissed and scuttled sideways.

"DADDDYYYYYY!" they all screeched in unison.
And just like that... Loki poofed in, mid-shave,
face half-lathered in clouds and panic.

"I... can explain."
They all ended up in a cozy dining room deep in
some forgotten realm.
Loki had never mentioned this particular
domestic dimension before, or his ex-wife,
Merrith of the Molten Isles, a sea-fire witch who
cooked emotion into food.

"So this is the best friend," Merrith said, stirring a
pot that smelled like unresolved tension and
oregano.

Aurelya smiled tightly. "Nice to meet you. Loki's
told me... nothing."

Loki choked on a breadstick.

The kids stared like they were watching a live
play.

"Do you love him?" asked the smallest one, wide-
eyed.

"Is he your soul-bond?" asked another.
"Did you come to take him away forever and doom us to therapy?"

Aurelya cleared her throat. "No. No. And… possibly?"
Dinner was awkward.

Merrith served "Regret Soup" and "Emotional Luggage Pie."
Loki tried to pretend it was fine by loudly discussing interdimensional politics.

"Remember that time you abandoned me during a cosmic thunderstorm?" Merrith asked, smiling sweetly.
"Aurelya, would you like more wine?"

Aurelya raised a brow. "Actually, I'd like answers."

The kids gasped.
So Loki confessed.

About the marriage.
The kids.
The years he tried to be something other than chaos and failed in spectacular, lovable fashion.

Aurelya listened.
Not with jealousy.
But with a quiet ache for all the versions of him
she would never know.

"Do you still love her?" she asked gently.

Loki stared at the table. Then shook his head.

"No. I never loved anyone like I love you."

The kids rallied behind Aurelya by dessert.

They made her a crown of spaghetti.
One offered her a pet eel.
The hissy one drew her in crayon, titled: "Queen
of Not-Yelling."

Merrith gave her a look at the end. A respectful
one.
"Take care of him. And make him do the
emotional work. I already gave him the starter
kit."

"I will," Aurelya said. "And thank you… for being
a real part of his story."
Back in their own realm, Aurelya curled up next
to Loki.

"You're a lot," she whispered.

"I know," he said. "But I'm all yours… if you'll have me."

Want to roll into Side Adventure #4: The Lion's Solo Journey to Learn How to Roar Again next? It's emotional, empowering, and a little heartbreaking.

Side Adventure Four: The Lion's Solo Journey to Learn How to Roar Again

Starring: The Lion (soft, brave, broken), a silent realm made of memory, and a voice that had been quiet for too long.

The Lion hadn't spoken in days.

Not a growl.

Not a purr.

Not even that little huff he made when Aurelya braided flowers into his mane and pretended it didn't make him tear up.

His roar had gone missing.

Not lost just… buried.

Beneath guilt, exhaustion, and the quiet heartbreak of always being the protector and never the protected.

So, one night, without telling anyone, he left.

He walked across moon-silver dunes, through forests made of whispers, until he reached the edge of the Realm of Remembering.

A place where memories echo.

And names have weight.

And silence is not absence; it's a question waiting to be answered.

The first thing he heard… was his own voice.
Young. Pure. Roaring like thunder in a field of stars.

Then… the day he failed.
The day a child cried, and he couldn't save them.
The day he froze and blamed himself forever after.
"You are only brave when you protect," the echo told him.
"When you lose… You are nothing."
He growled low. "That's not true."
The memory hissed back. "Then roar. Prove it."
He tried.
His throat shook.
But no sound came.
He wandered deeper.
Saw visions of every moment he had stood tall while trembling inside.
Every time he put on courage like armour, while his heart begged for rest.
He met an older lion, made of stars and scars.
"I lost my roar, too," the old one said. "Thought it meant I lost my purpose."
"Did you get it back?" the Lion asked.
"No. I made a new one."
The Lion stood on a cliff.
Beneath him, every version of himself.
Roaring. Crying. Failing. Loving.

Holding Aurelya when she couldn't stand.
Letting Loki curl against him when grief struck
without warning.
Staying soft when the world demanded claws.
He closed his eyes.
"I am not my mistakes."
"I am not my volume."
"I am not only worthy when I win."
Then he opened his mouth…
And this time, he didn't try to roar.
He sang.
Low. Ancient. A sound that trembled the stars.
A roar born not from rage but healing.
When he returned, Aurelya wept.
Loki tried to say, "You're back," but choked on it
and pretended he had sand in his eye.
The Lion smiled.
Didn't say a word.
But the way his presence filled the room?
It was louder than any roar.

Chapter Twenty-Two: The Realm That Knew Her Name Before She Spoke It

Starring: Aurelya (celestial and suddenly hunted), Loki (armed with mischief and panic), the Lion (silent but watching), and a realm that remembers too much.

They didn't mean to land there.
No portal was opened. No spell was cast.
It called her.
One moment, they were tracking a sun-fragment across the shattered river of Ymir's Vein.
The next?

They were standing in a place where the stars whispered in a language she hadn't heard since before her wings grew.
"This place wasn't on the map," Loki said, eyes narrowed.
"That's because it isn't a place," the Lion rumbled. "It's a memory given form."
The sky above them pulsed with soul light, fragments of memory flickering like constellations. But they weren't just anyone's

memories.
They were hers.

Childhood dreams she'd forgotten.
The sound of her laughter before the fall of the
first realm.
Her name the true one, not Aurelya, but the one
written on her soul.

And the realm knew it.
Suddenly, voices rose like smoke from the earth.

"She has returned."
"The one who left the gate open."
"The traitor, the exile, the seed of change…"
Aurelya froze.

"I didn't open the gate," she whispered. "I was
only a child."

"But you were the key," the voices said. "And
now you've come back. And the balance has
already begun to tilt."
Loki stepped between her and the voices.

"She owes you nothing."

"She owes everything."

From the shadows emerged the Witnesses, beings cloaked in star-ink and grief. They had no faces. Only masks. And names carved into their chests, names that shouldn't be spoken.
One mask turned to Aurelya.

"You were not supposed to survive.
And yet here you are.
With wings. With light. With them."
Suddenly, the stars screamed.
The realm began to fracture not with fire or violence… but truth.
Aurelya fell to her knees as memory flooded her:

The gate. The light. The voice that said: Run, and don't look back.
And she ran.
And she never stopped.
But the Lion caught her.
Wrapped his body around her like a shield of warmth and heartbeat and trust.
And for the first time… he spoke, softly.
"You are not your past.
You are not their judgment.
And you are not alone."

And as the stars shivered… she reached for her sword.
It glowed with her name now. The real one. Not

Aurelya.
Not yet spoken aloud but known.
"If you want to finish what was started," she said,
standing, "you'll have to get through all three of
us."
The stars held their breath.

Up Next: Aurelya's true story begins to awaken.
The Lion at her side. Loki holding back, for once.
The stars whispering secrets no one was meant
to remember.

Chapter Twenty-Three: The Memory That Was Buried Too Deep

Starring: Aurelya (on the edge of knowing), the Lion (ready to catch her again), Loki (for once, silent), and a door made of starlight that only opens for the truth.

The Witnesses didn't move. They simply… waited.

As if they knew she wouldn't strike. Not yet. Because something inside her had started to tremble not in fear, but in recognition.

Aurelya stared up at the broken sky. The stars weren't stars anymore.

They were memories.

And one of them was calling her name.

"Don't touch it," Loki warned softly.

"I have to," she whispered.

And she stepped forward into the light.

She was no longer in the realm. She stood in a corridor of sky black as sorrow, lined with ancient constellations rearranging themselves into moments.

The floor was not solid. It was memory shaped like marble, trembling beneath her feet.

She saw herself. Smaller. Wings not yet grown. Hair like fire. Eyes too wide.

Running. Through a corridor made of crystal. Behind her a gate. Sealed in vines of gold. Runes burned above it:

"DO NOT OPEN. DO NOT LET HER IN."

But someone had. And that someone…

"Aurelya," a voice said.

She turned. He was waiting.

He stood tall, in robes of woven midnight. A crown that bled moonlight. Eyes like gravity warm and ancient and heavy with knowing.

The god who told her to run.

"You shouldn't be here," he said.

"You told me to go," she said, her voice suddenly that of the child she was.

"Because if you had stayed… you'd be dead. Or worse obedient."

Aurelya's throat tightened.

"What was behind the gate?"

"You." he said simply. "Or the version of you they wanted."

"A weapon?"

"No. A vessel. Empty. Beautiful. Loyal."

She swallowed.

"So, I ran. But I forgot."

He stepped forward.

"You forgot because I made you forget. I took your name, your history, your flame and hid them in the stars. Because I loved you more than I feared the cost."

"What was the cost?"

The corridor darkened. His face crumbled.

"Me.

The image shattered like starlight on water. She gasped falling caught by the Lion's arms in the present.

Back in the real realm. The Witnesses watching.

She opened her eyes.

And she remembered:

Her real name. The god who loved her. The gate she never should have seen. And why the stars cry her name like a warning.

"What did you see?" Loki asked.

"The truth," she whispered. "And now… I need to find him."

"Who?" the Lion asked.

"The one who erased me. The one who saved me. The one who gave up everything so I could burn bright."

She turned to the Witnesses.

"You want the girl who opened the gate? You're too late. She ran. But I… I returned. And I'm not afraid of the truth anymore."

Up Next: Chapter 24 Flashback: The Day the Gate Was Opened We'll see the entire event unfold who opened it, what was inside, and why they feared Aurelya more than the realms themselves.

Chapter Twenty-Four: The Day the Gate Was Opened

Starring: Young Aurelya (not yet broken), the Hidden God (whose love defied fate), the Celestial Council (who wanted obedience), and the first time the Lion ever saw her.

Before she was Aurelya... Before she had wings... She was simply a child of starlight, born between realms, raised in shadows, and told never to ask why.

The Citadel was cold that day.

Not physically. But in the way marble halls feel when power outweighs truth. The Celestial Council had gathered.

Twelve beings. Twelve lies.

In the center of the chamber stood the Gate. Carved from cosmic bone. Locked by runes not meant to be seen.

And in front of it... a girl. No older than twelve. Eyes wide. Barefoot. Flanked by masked handlers.

"She's ready," one said. "She's compliant," said another. "She won't remember a thing," said the third.

But behind a curtain of veils, someone else was watching.

He wasn't part of the council. He was a god whose name had been erased from the records. A traitor in the making. A protector already.

"She's not ready," he whispered. "She's not theirs."

They began the ritual.

They spoke in ancient tongue.

They called it an "unlocking." But it was a severing. Her will, her spark, her future all to be hollowed out and filled with what the Council wanted:

A perfect vessel. A child who would obey. A tool they could wield.

But then…

He moved.

He shattered the sigils. Rushed into the light. Grabbed her, so small, so stunned and whispered into her ear:

"Run, Aurelya. Run and never look back. Don't let them write your ending."

"But… where?" she asked.

"Anywhere I'm not," he said with tears in his voice. "Because if I see you again, they'll kill you through me."

And then he did the impossible:

He gave up his name. His station. His right to the stars.

To erase himself from her memory to keep her free.

And she ran. Down the marble corridor. Through fire and glass. Her feet bleeding. Her breath wild.

Somewhere far below, in the gardens of the lower realms, a lion cub looked up. He heard the gate scream. He saw a girl fall from the sky, light pouring from her back.

She crash-landed in front of him.

"Are you real?" she asked, shaking.

"I think so," he said. "Are you?"

"Not anymore."

That day, he became her shadow. Even when she didn't remember why. Even when she forgot herself.

He followed her across realms. Quiet. Fierce. Waiting.

For the moment, she'd rise again.

Back in the present...

Aurelya opened her eyes.

And the Lion looked at her differently. Like he knew. Like he had always known.

"You were there," she whispered. "You saw me fall."

He nodded once.

"And I've been waiting for you to fly ever since."

Up Next: Chapter 25

Face the Witnesses. Unleash Aurelya with her full memory. And maybe just maybe the Lion takes his first step toward naming himself... Ready?

Chapter Twenty-Five: The Return of the Winged Flame

Starring: Aurelya (awakened), the Lion (rising), Loki (terrified but supportive), and the Witnesses who finally understand what they've summoned.

The realm hadn't changed.
But she had.
No longer trembling. No longer confused.
Aurelya stood tall, her wings fully outstretched, not ethereal and decorative as before, but now lit with burning runes that pulsed with ancient memory.
The stars bowed.
The wind bent around her form like it recognised a command.
And the Witnesses, cloaked in masks and judgment, began to take a collective step back.
"You're not supposed to exist," one whispered.
"She was meant to be erased," said another.
"You don't belong here," spat a third.
Aurelya's eyes burned like twin Novas.
"Then make me leave."

The Witnesses surged forward, no longer speaking, only screaming.

Reality around them twisted:
Shadow turned solid. Memory turned to ash.
They came not as individuals, but as a wave of
oblivion.
"Fall with the rest of your failures!" the largest
one howled, raising a staff made of forgotten
timelines.
And then he stopped.
Because standing in front of her now, unmoving.
was the Lion.

He hadn't roared.
Hadn't growled.
Hadn't spoken.
But his body had moved without hesitation
shield between Aurelya and death itself.
The ground quaked beneath his paws.
His muscles rippled.
His breath slowed.
"You will not touch her," he said, voice low. "Not
now. Not ever."

One of the Witnesses laughed.

"And who are you, beast? What name do you
wear? What history do you have?"
And the Lion paused.
Looked over his shoulder.
Saw Aurelya's hand rest softly against his side.

And he breathed out.
"I was once a cub who watched a goddess fall."
"And I have walked beside her ever since."
"You want my name?"
"I am Kaelun.
Born of silence.
Forged in shadow.
I am her roar when she cannot.
I am the storm at her side.
And today, I remember who I am."

The sky split.
Not with fire but with light.
Loki stepped forward, eyes wide. "Oh, that's new."

Aurelya: "Kaelun."
Lion: "Yes."
Aurelya: "It suits you."

Together, they turned to face the Witnesses.
And in that moment, prophecy shattered.
The erased girl remembered.
The silent lion roared.
The world that tried to forget them…
remembered everything.

Up Next Chapter 26

Time to lift the veil and expose the truth, even the gods were too afraid to say out loud.

Chapter Twenty-Six: What Lies Behind the Gate

Starring: Aurelya (awakened but not yet whole), Kaelun (the Lion reborn), Loki (connecting dots no one else wants to), and the Witnesses… finally breaking their silence.

The air fractured.
Not with magic but with history.
Truth peeling itself open like old wallpaper in a forgotten temple.
The Witnesses didn't strike again.
They simply… stood still.
Silent.
Their masks began to crack not from force, but from time.
And one by one, they removed them.
Underneath were faces like hers.
Eyes like starlight. Skin etched with memory scars.
Not enemies. Not monsters.
But survivors.
"You think we judged you," said the First.
"But we were you," said the Second.
"Each of us once wore wings. Each of us opened a gate. Each of us… ran."
Aurelya's breath caught.

"You… you were vessels too."

They nodded.

"We were the first. The prototypes. Some of us broke the Mold. Some of us burned. But we all paid the price for stepping outside their design."

Loki stepped forward, voice soft.

"You weren't Witnesses. You were warnings."

"We became what we had to," said the Third. "To make sure no other child wandered in unaware."

Kaelun growled. "Then why attack?"

"We weren't attacking. We were testing. We needed to know if she was whole. If her fire was her own or theirs."

The last Witness removed her mask.

Her face was older. Wiser. Familiar.

Aurelya whispered, "…Mother?"

"No," the woman said. "But I was once the one tasked with raising you. Before you escaped. Before he stole you from our program."

"The Hidden God?"

"He wasn't always hidden. He was our finest creation. Until he saw you… and chose love over loyalty."

Silence again.

And then:

The ground opened not violently, but with reverence.

Beneath the realm…
Beneath the memories…
Lay the true Gate. The final one.
And behind it?
Not power.
Not darkness.
Not war.
But a cradle of starlight.
A throne made of song.
And something… breathing.
Not alive in the mortal sense but ancient.
Dormant.
Waiting.
"This is what we tried to bury," said the Elder
Witness. "This is what we shaped you for."
"Not to be a weapon.
Not to be a ruler.
But a key."

Aurelya stepped forward.
Kaelun at her side.
Loki, whispering spells of protection.
And the Gate began to respond.
The runes glowed with her heartbeat.
The song rose with her breath.
"If I open it…" she asked, "what wakes?"
The Elder Witness smiled faintly.
"The rest of you."

Up Next Chapter 27: Want to find out what happens next? You will have to keep reading...

Chapter Twenty-Seven: The Cradle at the Centre of the Cosmos

But Not Yet Opened.
Starring: Aurelya (gathering herself), Kaelun (the shield becoming a sword), Loki (absolutely freaking out but pretending he's fine), and the ancient whispers of a past not yet done unravelling.

The Gate pulsed.
It knew her.
It wanted her.
Each beat echoed in her chest like the heartbeat of something both holy and horrifying.
She stepped forward
Then stopped.
"Not yet," she whispered.
The Witnesses said nothing.
They just bowed their heads.
Even they weren't ready for what came next.

That night, in the ruins of a temple carved from fallen star-metal, they made camp.

No one spoke for a long time.
Even Loki, who could joke through apocalypse,
sat quiet.
Finally, Aurelya broke the silence.
"If I open that gate, I lose the right to not know.
To not remember everything."
Kaelun looked up from where he was sharpening
his claws, a rhythm as calming to him as
breathing.
"And if you don't?" he asked.
"Then I stay half-born.
Half-fire.
Half-free."

She wandered outside, bare feet pressing into
glowing moss.
The air hummed with old stories.
Loki followed.
"You don't have to do this alone," he said, gently.
"I know," she replied. "But I think... to face it, I
have to stand still long enough to feel it. All of it."
"That sounds awful," he said, nudging her with
his elbow. "You sure I can't talk you into one last
distraction? We could go prank a storm giant.
Start a small cult. Bake cookies laced with
prophecy."
She smiled. "Maybe after."
He paused. Then:
"What if what's behind that gate... rewrites you?"

"Then I'll rewrite it back."
Inside the temple, Kaelun sat with a map of
realms spread out before him.
Old enemies. Old allies. Places they'd need to
visit before returning to the Gate.
"She needs strength," he murmured. "Not power.
Memory. Roots. Fire from more than just
herself."
He looked up at the sky.
And for the first time in years… he prayed.
That night, the stars didn't whisper.
They waited.
Because something ancient was stirring
But not from within the Gate.
From within her. Next stop:
They begin their journey across the Realms of
Reflection,
Memory, and Flame.
Each will give Aurelya a piece of herself back,
and each will test her in ways the Gate never
could.
Shall we start with Chapter 28: The Realm of
Mirrors? Where must Aurelya face the version of
herself that never ran the obedient vessel she
might've become?

Chapter Twenty-Eight: The Realm of Mirrors

Starring: Aurelya (bracing), Kaelun (watching),
Loki (wearing sunglasses indoors), and a version
of herself who never escaped the Gate.

They crossed the threshold at dawn.
The Realm of Mirrors shimmered on the horizon,
not made of glass, but of possibility.
It was said to reflect not your appearance…
…but the version of yourself you almost became.
As they stepped inside, the air thickened.
The sky turned silver.
The ground gleamed like frozen water but
shifted with every step.
And then the first mirror rose up from the mist.
"Is that… me?" Aurelya asked.
"Not you," Kaelun said. "A branch. A could-have.
A never-was."
The figure inside the mirror stood tall. Regal.
Her wings were clipped at the top, not broken,
but sculpted into a perfect curve.
Her eyes were empty. Her smile flawless.
She wore a crown of obedience.
She was everything the Council tried to make
her.

"Welcome, Aurelya," the mirror-self said.
"You fled your fate. I fulfilled it.
You are chaos. I am peace."
"You're a puppet," Aurelya replied.
"You're a storm," the reflection countered.
Aurelya stepped closer. "And what are you guarding?"
The mirror cracked.
Just slightly.

Another mirror rose beside it.
Another version of her, this one aged. Wounded. Alone.
She had never escaped the Council... but had tried.
Had failed.
"This is the cost of disobedience," the older version rasped.
"Pain. Isolation. Being forgotten."
Aurelya trembled.
Kaelun stood behind her, silent.
"If you need me..."
"No," she said. "This is mine to face."
The final mirror rose like a monolith.
Inside it stood a version of her with no name.
No wings. No voice.
She sat in a white chamber, smiling endlessly at a wall.
No thoughts. No soul.

Just perfection.
"This is who they wanted me to be," Aurelya
whispered.
Loki gritted his teeth.
Kaelun's claws dug into the earth.
"Break it," the lion growled.
But Aurelya stepped forward instead…
…and touched the mirror.
The reflection looked up.
Eyes blank.
Aurelya whispered:
"I see you.
I'm sorry.
And I'm not going back."
The mirror shattered.
And when it did
Something rose from the shards.
A piece of her.

A glowing ember. A memory. A voice that once
said no and meant it.
She took it.
Held it to her chest.
And it sank into her like a puzzle piece finding its
place.

As they walked back toward the next realm,
Aurelya looked at her hands.
"What now?" Loki asked.

"Now," she said, "we find the next version of me they tried to bury."
End of Chapter 28.

Next up: Chapter 29: The Realm of Flame where Aurelya must reclaim her rage the power, they told her was dangerous… because it was.
Ready to walk through fire?

Chapter Twenty-Nine: The Realm of Flame

Starring: Aurelya (finally ready to burn), Kaelun (on guard), Loki (concerned but deeply impressed), and the forgotten fury that was never meant to be hers... but always was.

The entrance to the Realm of Flame didn't burn.
It waited.
The air was still.
The sky glowed ember-orange.
The heat didn't scorch it seduced.
This was not a land of wildfire.
This was controlled combustion.
Fire kept in chains.
"They brought me here once," Aurelya murmured, standing at the threshold.
"To test me. To tame me."
Kaelun stepped beside her, shoulder brushing hers.
"Did it work?"
"No. But I pretended it did. That was worse."

As they crossed the threshold, the world shifted.
The ground was black glass, cracked and smoking.
Floating above the molten horizon were embers

shaped like memories, each flickering with emotion she had swallowed instead of expressed.
Pain.
Injustice.
Betrayal.
Rage.

"Where's the test?" Loki asked.
The fire answered.
It rose.
All around them. A sudden wall. A ring of heat and fury.
Aurelya stood in the centre, the flames licking toward her, not to burn… but to tempt.
A voice rose from the fire:
"You've earned the right to unleash."
"Let us burn for you.
She saw visions in the flames:
  • The Council robbing her name.
  • The Witnesses judging her.
  • That blank-eyed version of herself in the mirror.
The fire whispered:
"Let go.
Tear the stars down.
You were made to be feared."

Kaelun tried to move, but the fire held him back.

Loki called out, "Aurelya, don't lose yourself!"
But she stood, eyes closed, arms wide.
And said:
"I'm not here to destroy the world.
I'm here to destroy the lie."
And with that, she stepped into the heart of the
fire.

The ground split.
The flames roared.
And from within them, she screamed.
Not in pain.
But in power.
A scream for every time she'd silenced herself.
For every "be good," "stay small," "don't shine
too bright."
It was a roar of becoming.

When the flames died down, she stood their eyes
golden.
Hair wild.
A crown of flickering embers forming behind her
head like a halo of rebellion.
In her hand: a new weapon.
A blade of living flame, shaped like a phoenix's
wing.
"This time," she said, "I burn for me."

Next up: Chapter 30: The Realm of Memory, the final stop before returning to the Cradle Gate.
This one, she'll have to face the Hidden God himself…
And what he gave up to save her.
Ready?

Chapter Thirty: The Realm of Memory

Starring: Aurelya (armoured in fire and clarity), Kaelun (always watching), Loki (unusually quiet), and the Hidden God, the one who loved her enough to disappear.

The Realm of Memory was not a place.
It was a threshold.
A slow descent into starlight...
And then into silence.
There were no walls.
No sky.
No up, no down.
Only moments, suspended like lanterns in the dark.
And at the centre, glowing faintly, was his memory.
The god who told her to run.
The one who had erased himself so she could survive.
The one who may have loved her more than fate allowed.

They stepped into the lantern.
Time folded.
And suddenly... they were there.

The chamber was small. Private.
Made of black glass and fading spells.
He stood at the edge, cloaked in deep midnight.
A golden thread coiled between his fingers, her thread. Her name.
The one he had severed.
He didn't turn.
But he knew she was there.
"You weren't supposed to find this," he said softly.
"But I did," Aurelya replied.
"Because you're stronger than I hoped," he whispered. "And because I was foolish enough to think you'd stay hidden forever."

She stepped forward.
Her flame didn't burn this realm.
It flickered gently like grief.
"Why did you do it?" she asked.
"Because the Council didn't want a daughter.
They wanted a symbol.
Something pure. Obedient. Hollow."
"I could've fought."

"You shouldn't have had to," he said, turning at last.
His face was older now.
Lined with knowing.
Eyes like the beginning of stars.

"I loved you," he said. "Before they chose what you'd become.
So I broke the story. I broke me.
To give you a chance to write your own."
Silence hung between them.
Then Aurelya stepped closer, placed her hand over his heart.
"I didn't remember you," she said. "But somewhere inside me… I missed you."
"That's enough," he whispered.
He raised his hand. Touched her cheek.
"You're not the child I saved anymore."
"No," she said. "I'm the woman who's coming back to finish what you started."
And then he faded.
Not with sadness but with peace.
Because she didn't need him to protect her anymore.
She was her own flame now.

Kaelun was waiting as she stepped back into the present.
Loki, eyes misted, handed her a napkin.
"That was awful," he said. "Also, beautiful. I hate this. I'm crying."
She laughed. Just once. But it was real.
And then she looked at them both.
"Let's go back to the Gate."

Next chapter:
Chapter 31 – The Gate Opens
Everything she has remembered, claimed,
earned it leads to this.
The cradle. The truth. The final choice.
Shall we?

Chapter Thirty-One: The Gate Opens

Starring: Aurelya (complete), Kaelun (the roar at her side), Loki (armed with sarcasm and unshakable loyalty), and the secret that even the gods feared to name.

The Gate didn't greet her.
It recognised her.
As she stepped into the realm again, fire in her heart, memory in her bones, Kaelun and Loki at her side, the Gate shimmered like a sleeping breath.
The Witnesses stood back.
They didn't speak.
They simply watched.
Because they knew.
This was no longer about prophecy.
This was not about rebellion.
This was the moment the world tilted.

Aurelya raised her hand.
Her fingers glowed not just with flame or light but with story.
The kind that had been cut out of history.
The kind too dangerous to remember.

The runes on the Gate pulsed.

Each one responding to a different version of her:

- The girl who ran.
- The woman who burned.
- The goddess who returned.

"This is your last chance to turn back," Kaelun said gently.

"I know," Aurelya replied. "And I won't."

"Do we have a plan?" Loki asked.

"Nope," she said. "Just courage."

"…Well, that's new."

She placed her hand on the Gate.

It sang.

Not loud.

Not violent.

Just a quiet, perfect harmony.

Then… it opened.

Not with thunder.

Not with light.

But with stillness.

Inside was not fire, nor power, nor doom.

It was a cradle.

Floating in starlight.

Carved from the bones of the first realm.

Inside it not a baby.

But a flame.

Pure. Ancient.
Flickering.
Alive.
"What is that?" Loki whispered.
Kaelun stepped forward.
His eyes narrowed.
"That's not a weapon," he said. "That's a soul."
Aurelya stepped closer.
And the flame… rose.
It hovered before her.
And then, like wind to a candle, it merged with her.

No pain.
Just warmth.
Welcome home, it said in her voice.

Her eyes closed.

And in that moment, she saw everything.
The first spark that created her.
The gods who feared her.
The real reason they sealed her away.
She wasn't a threat to the world.
She was a threat to the story.
Because if she lived, if she chose her path,
then everyone else could too.

No more fate.
No more chosen ones.
No more locked gates.
Just freedom.

She opened her eyes.
Her wings were brighter now.
Her aura, wider.
Her voice when she spoke was the kind of sound
that makes gods kneel.
"I remember now.
And I choose not to be anyone's prophecy."

Up Next: The Epilogue…

EPILOGUE: And the Stars Remembered Her Name

Somewhere far from the Gate,
a child looked up at the night sky...
and saw a new star.
It pulsed once.
Then again.
Like a heartbeat too ancient for time, too wild for
prophecy.

In the quiet between realms, the Council
gathered.
They spoke in hushed tones.
Of breaches.
Of awakening.
Of her.
"It cannot be undone," one whispered.
"We should have sealed her completely," another
hissed.
"We tried," murmured the eldest. "But you
cannot bind fire with rules. And you cannot cage
a soul that remembers it was born free."
They fell silent.
Because somewhere deep in the void,
a flame had lit a path they could no longer
control.

In the Realm of the Cradle, the Gate now stood open forever.

Aurelya sat beside it, watching the light ripple.

Kaelun lay nearby, his breath slow, steady.

Guarded. Always.

Loki?

Wrote "DO NOT TOUCH" signs and taped them to every pillar of stardust he could find.

"You're going to change everything, you know," he said.

"Good," Aurelya replied. "It's long overdue."

She looked into the vastness of the cosmos.

Not with fear.

Not with uncertainty.

But with readiness.

Because the world didn't need a vessel.

It needed a voice.

And she was done whispering.

The End of Book One.

Aurelya has awakened.

Kaelun has remembered.

Loki is… still Loki.

And far across the stars, something old has begun to stir…

The End of Book One.
Book One of the Realm Shatter Saga

Bonus Peek: The Flame Continues…

Aurelya may have survived the Gate… but something far older and far pettier just woke up.

In the next book, a gala turns into cosmic chaos, and Loki may or may not be banned from buffet tables.
And a flame Aurelya thought she'd left behind comes roaring back.

So… what happens when a newly awakened goddess crashes a divine reunion with hors d'oeuvres?
Let's find out.

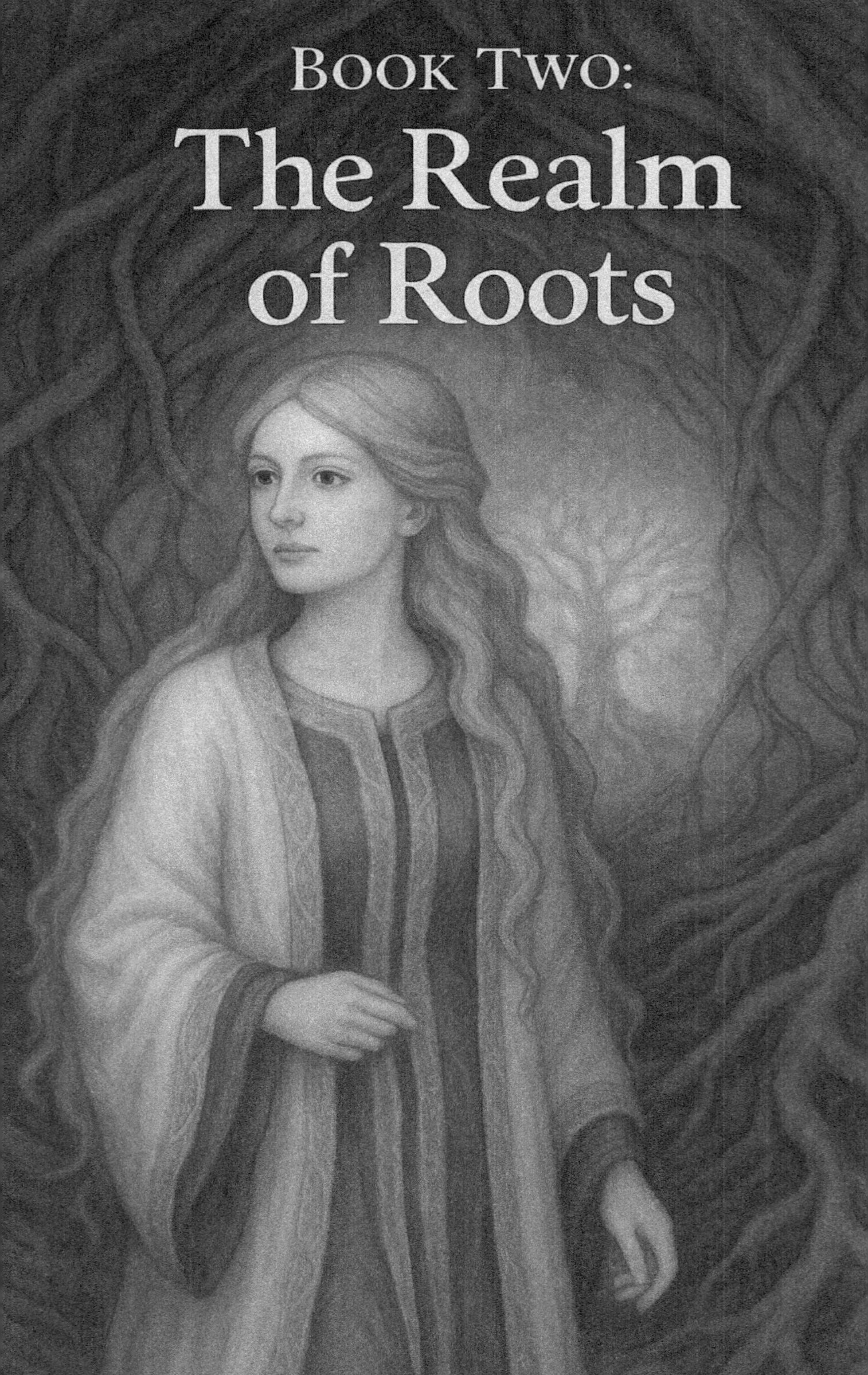

BOOK TWO:
The Realm
of Roots

Volume 2: The Realms Reclaim Her

Book 2

• Book 2: The Realm of Roots, she reconnects with her ancestry, forgotten bloodlines, and the oldest truth: she is not the first flame.

OFFICIAL INVITATION FROM THE DESK OF

LADY FRAYA

ETERNAL QUEEN OF THE 10TH REALM

YOU ARE SUMMONED

to attend the inaugural

Gala of Glorious Reclamation

hosted by Fraya, High Lady of
Boundaries, Sass, and Survivorsship,
on the occasion of:

- THE DRAMATIC (AND OVERDUE) AWAKENING
  OF AURELYA, FLAME-CHILD OF THE COSMOS

- ODIN'S EXTENDED NATURE NAP ON DAY 9
  (HE'S STILL TIED TO A TREE, IT'S FINE)

- THE OFFICIAL RELAUNCH OF THE TENTH
  REALM AS A SANCTUARY FOR GODDESSES,
  LIONS, DRAGONS, AND EMOTIONALLY

Official Invitation from the Desk of Lady Fraya,
Eternal Queen of the 10th Realm

YOU ARE SUMMONED
to attend the inaugural
Gala of Glorious Reclamation

hosted by Fraya, High Lady of
Boundaries, Sass, and Survivorship,
on the occasion of:

- The dramatic (and overdue) awakening of
  Aurelya, Flame-Child of the Cosmos
- Odin's extended nature nap on Day 9 (he's
  still tied to a tree, it's fine)
- The official relaunch of the Tenth Realm as a
  sanctuary for goddesses, lions, dragons, and
  emotionally available men (all zero of them]

DATE:
The Night the Stars Finally Snap
(or this Thursday)

LOCATION:
The 10th Realm (now under new management)

Coordinates available by starlight only. Wear shoes that float.

DRESS CODE:
- Divine
- Dramatic
- Deeply Disrespectful to Your Former Captors

Note: If your outfit doesn't scare at least one archangel, you're underdressed.

FEATURED HIGHLIGHTS:
- Aurelya's Dragon debuts its first attempt at culinary arts (waivers required)
- Kaelun the Lion tries sparkling nectar. What could go wrong?
- Loki's Squirrel will be performing unauthorised stand-up, followed by a disappearing act that may involve your wallet.
- Thor's chickens will not be on the menu but may demand a ceremonial fight pit.

RSVP (Required. Or Else.):
Please respond via celestial rune, goat courier, or loud interpretive dance in the direction of Asgard.

This is not a peace summit. This is a reckoning.
Come dressed to slay, dance, or accidentally start
a minor divine conflict.

And remember:
Revenge is a dish best served with champagne
and your ex's stolen war helm.

With delight and veiled menace,
Fraya

Fraya

Eternal Hostess, Still Waiting for Odin to
Apologise

Chapter One: The Gala Begins (Someone Please Save the Tapas)

Aurelya had fought divine bureaucracy.
She had faced her mirror-self.
She had awakened her soul at the centre of the
cosmos.

But nothing, nothing, could have prepared her
for this party.

The 10th Realm had changed.

No longer forgotten.
No longer forbidden.
Now it glowed with defiance, high towers
braided
with light, floating lanterns shaped like side-
eyes, and
A red carpet of stardust trailed up to the gates,
flanked by two celestial flamingos wearing
earrings.

Loki stood at the entrance, sunglasses on, scroll

in hand, fur collar definitely stolen.

"Names?" he asked dramatically.

Aurelya arched a brow. "Really?"

"Look, if we let in everyone, the emotional
support raccoons will start another conga line."

Inside, the ballroom shimmered like liquid
moonlight.
At the centre: Fraya, dripping in gold and wrath,
sipping a drink made of fire and glitter.

She spotted Aurelya and lit up like a satisfied
prophecy.

"There she is! My cosmic phoenix!"
"I brought my lion," Aurelya said.
"Of course you did," Fraya smiled. "Every
goddess needs a living metaphor."
Meanwhile...
Kaelun stood awkwardly near a buffet table,
staring suspiciously at a bowl of glowing jelly
cubes that were humming softly.
"Are they... singing?" he asked.
"Don't eat those," said a passing elf. "Last guy bit
one and hasn't stopped breakdancing since."

The dragon, curled around the punch fountain, was wearing a frilly apron and breathing just enough fire to flambé the hors d'oeuvres.

"I made pie," it growled proudly.
"Is it… safe?"
"Mostly."
"For eating or for weaponising?"
"Yes."

Then chaos struck.

Ratatoskr, Loki's squirrel, burst onto the chandelier, wielding a cheese knife and screaming:

"NO ONE TOUCHES THE GOUDA! IT IS MINE, YOU DIVINE PEASANTS!"

Loki sighed. "He gets like this during retrogrades."
Thor entered last.

He was radiant.
Triumphant.
And absolutely surrounded by chickens.

"BEHOLD!" he bellowed. "MY ELVEN-FORGED

CHICKEN ARMADA!"

Tiny battle helmets. Enchanted feathers.
One of them carried a miniature axe.

"They play Warhammer," Thor said proudly.
"With real war. And also hammers."

The music swelled.
The food trembled.
The squirrel screamed.
Aurelya laughed so hard she cried.

And for a moment, just one, there was no
prophecy.
No fear.
No gate.

Just warmth.
And weirdness.
And chosen family.

But far above the realm...
In the cracks between stars...

Something old was watching.

And it had not been invited.

Next up:

Chapter Two – The Cracks Begin to Spread
...as the Gala gets interrupted by something far
worse than an undercooked dragon pie.
Ready?

Chapter Two: The Cracks Begin to Spread

Starring: Aurelya (finally laughing), Kaelun (suspicious), Loki (lying, probably), Thor (preparing chicken battalions), and Something That Shouldn't Exist

It happened just as Fraya dramatically announced the "Cleansing of the Exes" course of the meal which featured roasted narcissism, glazed disrespect, and one flaming dish named Regret Flambé.
The chandeliers dimmed.
The laughter paused.
Aurelya turned her head slightly.
The stars were flickering.
Not fading glitching.

"That's not supposed to happen," Loki muttered, pulling a rune from his sleeve and scanning the

ceiling like a dad checking storm clouds at a barbecue.
Kaelun stepped away from the wall.
His claws echoed softly on the marble.
"I smell... realm rot," he growled.
"What's that?" Thor asked, hand on chicken.

"It's when reality forgets how to hold itself together," Kaelun replied.

"Like my cousin Eirik on tequila," Thor nodded solemnly.

Aurelya walked to the centre of the ballroom.
The air was buzzing like static. Like interference.
And then
The wall behind her cracked open.
Not like stone.
Like fabric tearing at the seams.
Behind it?
Not darkness.
Not fire.
Just... absence.
A void so quiet it hurt.
Out of it came a voice:
"There was only supposed to be one of you."
Aurelya's pulse stilled.
"Who's there?" she asked.
The voice laughed softly like a mirror warping.
"A correction."

The room exploded into panic.
Tables tipped.
Chickens screamed.
The dragon swallowed a candle and belched fireworks.
Loki threw a spoon at the void.

"WHY IS IT ALWAYS AT PARTIES?!"
Kaelun pulled Aurelya behind him.
"Get out of here," he said to Thor, "Take the animals."
"They have names," Thor said, indignant.
"Fine. Take Murder cluck and the others, just go."

But Aurelya didn't move.
She stepped toward the crack.
"What are you?" she asked.
The voice whispered back:
"What's left... when the story breaks."
And then the crack sealed itself shut.
Just like that.
Gone.
But something stayed behind.
On the floor.
Where the void had touched the realm.
A single white feather.
Made not of down.
But of bone.
End of Chapter Two.
Next up:
Interlude and then Chapter Three: The Feather That Wasn't Meant to Fall
Flash Back Interlude: The Watcher in the Void
Location: A fractured realm, long before Aurelya's awakening.

Time: Years before the events of Realm shatter.
Cast: Kaelun (alone), a dying realm, and a choice no one saw him make.

The wind here didn't howl.
It whispered.
Like the realm itself was trying not to wake the dead.
Kaelun knelt beside a pool of silver not water, but broken sky that had fallen inward. His claws hovered just above the surface.
This was the fourth realm to rot this cycle.
The fourth to forget how to hold itself together.
He closed his eyes.
Listened.
Not for sounds, but for the absence of them.
Silence real silence had weight.
The kind that settled in your bones and whispered it's too late.
He stood, shoulders broad and still, framed by what was left of the twilight.
And in the stillness, a memory stirred.
"You're not like the others," the old priest had told him, long ago, when Kaelun still flinched at his own reflection.
"You weren't born to fight. You were born to see it coming."
That had been a curse at first.
Then a weapon.

Now… just a burden.

Kaelun reached into his belt and pulled out a shard, obsidian laced with gold veins. A remnant from the first realm he'd failed to save.
He didn't cry. He hadn't in years.
But the ground did.
Cracks spidered out from where he stood, as if the realm itself recoiled from his presence.
"I warned them," he said aloud, though no one remained to hear it.
His voice didn't echo.
It never did in the places that were already breaking.
A faint glimmer caught his eye a feather, white as light… but edged in bone.
Kaelun narrowed his gaze.
He'd seen one like it before.
Only once.
And if it had returned?
So had the thing that left it behind.

Somewhere in the future… in a ballroom of laughter and glitching stars… Kaelun would smell realm rot again.

This time, he would not be too late.

Chapter Three – The Feather That Wasn't Meant to Fall

Starring: Aurelya (compelled), Kaelun (on edge), Loki (concerningly quiet), Thor (trying to train chickens to detect evil), and one bone-feather that hums like memory and rot.

They stared at it.
The ballroom was in shambles.
Chairs overturned. Spoons embedded in walls.
The dragon was hiccupping sparks.
The chickens had formed a protective circle around Thor and were now chanting in chicken.
But none of it mattered.
Because that feather didn't belong.
It didn't fall from a bird.
Or a beast.
Or a god.
It had no origin.
And that was the problem.

Aurelya approached first.
It hummed.
Not out loud but in her chest.
A low, aching hum, like a heartbeat turned inside out.

"It feels like… memory," she said softly.
"No," Loki said. "It feels like a rejection slip from the universe."
Kaelun growled.
"Don't touch it."
Aurelya touched it.

It shocked her.
Not with pain but with clarity.
And suddenly… she saw.
A vision:
A ruined realm.
Her realm?
No not yet.
But a future one.
Empty.
Drained.
And standing in the centre a figure.
Wings made of bone.
Eyes like holes in the sky.
And in its hand?
A sword carved from feathers just like this one.

Aurelya gasped and dropped the feather.
It hit the ground…
…and began to grow.

Kaelun lunged. Covered it with his paw.
Too late.

The feather curled in on itself, spun, and took shape.
A seed.
A seed of something that was never supposed to live.

"This isn't just a warning," Loki said, eyes wide. "It's a planted future."
"It's trying to root itself," Kaelun muttered.
"In what?" Aurelya asked.
Loki looked at her.
Then at the floor.
Then at all of them.
"In us."

The seed pulsed once.
And everyone felt it:
- Regret
- Shame
- A memory they swore they'd buried

This thing wasn't an object.
It was a story fragment the kind that rewrites you from the inside out.

"We have to take it," Aurelya said.
"Take it where?" Thor asked. "To the chicken bunker? To Fraya's spa realm? To"
"To where the Realms first cracked," Kaelun said.

"You mean" Loki began.

"Yes," Aurelya said. "We're going back to the Folded Realm."

Loki groaned.

"Great. Nothing like revisiting the broken bones of time while a ghost feather tries to eat our souls."

Next up:

Chapter Four Return to the Folded Realm
Where timelines bend, forgotten memories whisper, and one of the trios might not make it out the same.
Shall we?

Chapter Four: Return to the Folded Realm

Starring: Aurelya (bracing), Kaelun (guarded), Loki (deeply offended at being here), and the realm that breaks reality like glass under pressure.

The Folded Realm had many names:
  • The Scrapbook of Time
  • The Realm Between Versions
  • That One Place Where Reality Has a Panic Attack
It was where abandoned timelines curled up to die
where discarded versions of gods still wandered, asking, "Did I win? Did I love? Did I matter?"
It was also where Aurelya was almost erased.
And now they were going back.

"Remind me why this is a good idea?" Loki grumbled as they hovered outside the veil.
"Because the feather came from what's next," Aurelya said. "And this place… shows us what was almost."

"I hate when you make sense," Loki muttered, tucking emergency chocolate into his belt.

Kaelun said nothing.
He just stepped through the veil.

Inside, time was sideways.
Clouds drifted up.
Thoughts echoed before you had them.
And at the centre: a broken tower made of every
version of a life that had ever been unlived.

They entered carefully.
The seed now in a glass sphere pulsed slowly like
a heartbeat.
"Do we bury it here?" Aurelya asked.
"No," Kaelun said, sniffing the air. "We're not
alone."

Suddenly
A voice.
Familiar.
Unwelcome.
Too calm.
"Well, well, well... look who finally came back to
their own disaster."
From behind a crooked mirror stepped...
Aurelya.
But not this Aurelya.
This one wore chains made of light.
Her wings? Missing.
Her smile? Beautiful. Wrong.

“I did everything right,” Mirror-Aurelya said.
“I followed the Council. I saved the Realms.
And yet you… the one who ran… you get the
story?”
Aurelya froze.
“You’re a version of me?”
“I’m the version that stayed. That obeyed.
And I died for it.”
She stepped forward.

“Now it’s my turn to live.”

Kaelun growled.
Loki summoned a glowing spoon. (His magic was
not coping well here.)
“You’re not her,” Kaelun said.
“No,” Mirror-Aurelya whispered.
“But I remember what it felt like to be.
And that makes me dangerous.”

Suddenly, the seed cracked.
A thin, sharp white tendril crept from it reaching
toward Mirror-Aurelya like a root searching for
blood.
“Oh no,” Loki said. “Oh nope, nope, absolutely
not”
But it was too late.
She touched the tendril.
And merged with it.

The air screamed.
Time bent inward.
And standing where Mirror-Aurelya had been…
was something new.
Something hungry.
Something made of bone and light and what-ifs.

"You made your choice," it said in a voice that
echoed like every Aurelya that never was.
"Now face the consequences of being the one
who survived."

End of Chapter Four.

Next chapter:
Chapter Five: The Broken Version
Aurelya must fight the part of herself that
could've become the story's villain or maybe
already did.
Ready?

Chapter Five: The Broken Version

Starring: Aurelya (facing herself), Kaelun (ready to intervene), Loki (has a backup plan and a backup spoon), and the creature who knows her too well.

The thing that stood before them was not just a version of Aurelya.
It was what happens when a soul is silenced long enough to believe it should be.

It still looked like her… mostly.
But its eyes glowed with compliance.
Its spine arched like it was waiting for permission.
And its voice? Sweet. Sharp. Twisted.
"I died a hero, you know," it said. "I died saving the Realms.
And yet your story lives on. The wild one. The loud one.
The uncontrolled one."

Aurelya took a step forward.
"You were never supposed to die," she said quietly.
"None of us were.
We were supposed to live.
But they only let one of us do it."

"And you think you deserve that?" the Broken
Version hissed.
"You left. You burned everything down.
And they still made you the Flame."
Aurelya clenched her fists.
"No. I made me the Flame.
They tried to unmake me first."

Suddenly, the creature lunged not at Aurelya...
But at Kaelun.
"Take her lion, take her heart," it growled. "Let
her watch this version WIN."
Kaelun roared louder than the Realms had heard
in centuries and slammed the creature back with
a wave of protective force.
"You are not her," he growled. "You are what was
done to her."
Aurelya stepped between them.
No blade.
No spell.
Just her voice.
"You don't need to fight me," she said gently.
"You are me.
But you're stuck in the pain they made us carry."
"So, what do you suggest?" the creature snapped.
"A hug? A poem?"
Aurelya stepped forward.
And instead of attacking...
She held out her hand.

"I see you.
I forgive you.
But I won't let you grow in me."
The creature faltered.
Flickered.
And then
Cracked.
Like glass catching sunlight the wrong way.
It didn't scream.
It just whispered:
"Don't forget us."
Then shattered into stardust.
Leaving behind only a faint sound:
A child's voice saying thank you.

Loki exhaled like he'd been holding it for five chapters.
"That was either incredibly wise… or wildly unsafe."
Kaelun looked at Aurelya.
"Are you alright?"
She wiped her eyes.
"I'm not sure. But I think… I'm whole."
Behind them, the glass sphere with the seed stopped pulsing.
It had burned itself out.

The future it tried to plant?
Uprooted.

Next up:

Chapter Six: The Price of Being Whole

Because not everyone is thrilled that she survived this.

And someone new has just stepped into the Realms... claiming they were sent to stop her.

Shall we continue?

Chapter Six: The Price of Being Whole

Starring: Aurelya (cantered, for now), Kaelun (on edge), Loki (extremely suspicious), and a stranger who claims to know the end of her story before she does.

The Folded Realm fell silent.
No more echoes.
No more flickering lights.
The version that should never have been… was gone.

But in that silence, something *else* arrived.

A wind rose.

Not cold. Not warm.
Just… unfamiliar.

Kaelun's fur bristled.

Loki held up a hand, runes hovering like little nervous birds.

Then …
a footstep.
Deliberate.
Slow.
Too real for a place made of memory.

From the shifting horizon came a figure.

Tall.
Veiled.
Wearing robes woven from letters not yet
written.

Their voice?
Smooth. Measured.
Like someone *used to being believed.*

"Well done, Flame. You've passed the first
fracture."

"And you are?" Aurelya asked, not blinking.

"I am the Binder," they said.
"Sent from the End to observe the Thread that
resists erasure."
Loki made a face.

"Sent from the End? What are you, narrative tax agents?"

The Binder smiled.
"I keep records. I log deviations. I document…
anomalies."

"And me surviving is an anomaly?" Aurelya asked.

The Binder tilted their head.

"You weren't meant to.
And yet here you are reuniting versions,
rejecting implants,
daring to be whole."

Kaelun stepped forward.

"If she's a threat, say it."

"Oh, not a threat," The Binder replied.
"A *variable.*"

They waved a hand.

A flickering scroll appeared in the air showing
Aurelya's future.
Thousands of branching lines.
Some glowing.
Some charred.

One blinking violently.

"There is one path," The Binder said,
"Where you survive, save the Realms, and
ascend."

"Only one?" Aurelya asked.

"Yes. And the cost... is everything else."

The scroll vanished.

"Choose carefully, Flame," they said. "Not every
path is yours to keep."
And then
they disappeared.
No flash. No noise.
Just... gone.

The Realms settled again.
But the weight of what they'd seen

Pressed in.

"So," Loki said eventually, "how are we feeling on a scale from
1 to 'I'm a divine paradox that might unravel
time itself?'"

Aurelya looked at her hands.

They weren't glowing.

They were steady.
"I feel…
like I've finally started my story."

Next:
Chapter Seven – The Thread That Cuts Both
Ways
Aurelya begins seeing pieces of possible
futures… and must make a choice that might
undo her one safe bond:
Kaelun.

Ready?

Chapter Seven: The Thread That Cuts Both Ways

Starring: Aurelya (seeing too much), Kaelun (holding steady), Loki (trying to make jokes but definitely worried), and the first real tear in their unbreakable bond.

It began that night.

Not with thunder.
Not with fire.
But with a dream that *wasn't a dream.*

Aurelya saw Kaelun, bleeding.
Not from battle.
But from *abandonment.*

He stood alone on a broken battlefield calling her name, over and over,
as if she had *left him behind.*

She woke in tears.

The dream clung to her.

Not like a warning.

Like a preview.

"It's the feather," Loki said.
"The energy lingers. You touched it too long."

"It didn't just show me the future," she
whispered.
"It *implanted* them."

Over the next few days, they *kept coming.*
- Kaelun, turning away.
- Kaelun, calling her "monster."
- Kaelun… *gone.*

Each time, she woke with a pain in her chest like
a tether fraying.

But Kaelun?
Was still there.

Solid.
Steady.
Watching her with those eyes that always knew
when she was pretending to be fine.
Finally, she snapped.

"Why are you still here?!"

Kaelun blinked.
"What?"

"In every possible version I see you *leave me.*
So why haven't you yet?"

Kaelun stared for a moment, stunned.

Then, quietly:

"Because *this* version hasn't failed yet."

Aurelya broke.

"What if I become something I can't control?
What if the Binder's right and I *unravel
everything*?"

Kaelun stepped forward.

"Then I'll catch the pieces."

"And if I shatter you too?"
He touched her forehead gently with his.

"Then we break together.
And rebuild."

But deep inside…
Aurelya still felt it.

The thread.
Tugging.

A single decision in the future that would cut him
from her.
For the good of the realms.
For the cost of her heart.

Later, alone, Loki sat beside her.
"He doesn't know yet, does he?" he asked.

Aurelya shook her head.

"No.
But when it comes… I won't ask him to choose."

Loki was quiet.

Then, softly:

"That's the most brutal part of love, isn't it?
Letting them walk away clean…
when your heart's still bleeding all over their
footprints."

Next:
 Chapter Eight – Where the Past Begins to
Answer Back
They return to the root of the Tree Yggdrasil
where Day Nine left Odin scarred… and
something *buried* begins to stir.

Shall we descend?

Chapter Eight: Where the Past Begins to Answer Back

Starring: Aurelya (haunted), Kaelun (resolute), Loki (nervous), and Yggdrasil, the Tree that remembers too much.

They didn't speak as they travelled.

Even Loki, who could usually fill silence with seventeen inappropriate metaphors, kept quiet.

Because the base of Yggdrasil was not just sacred

it was dangerous.

The bark pulsed with ancient memory.

The roots twitched like nerves.

And beneath the surface?

Day Nine was still echoing.

They arrived just before dusk.

The light cut through the branches like golden blades.

And in the dirt, carved by hand, were the remnants of Odin's madness

scribbles, markings, a circle of blood.

Kaelun stared at them.

"This is where he broke, isn't it?" he asked.

Loki nodded.

"Day Nine. When the visions stopped showing him wisdom…

and started showing him truth."

Aurelya stepped forward.

Her wings flickered

not from power,

but from proximity.

"Something's buried here."

Kaelun crouched.

“Bone? Memory?”

“Both,” she whispered.

She touched the soil.

It recoiled.

And then, like a breath,
the ground opened.

What rose wasn’t an object.
It was a ghost of intention.

A memory so strong it had become real.

It looked like Odin.
But younger.
Desperate.
Cracked open from the inside.

"Don't look for me," it begged.

"Don't follow the roots.

They'll only show you where you never grew."

Aurelya reached out not to touch it, but to witness it.

Suddenly:

visions poured in.

• Odin begging the Norns to rewrite fate.

• Odin whispering a name he was never supposed to know.

• Odin striking a bargain under the tree, with something older than time.

She staggered back.

"He didn't sacrifice himself," she gasped.

"He traded."

Loki turned pale.

"For what?"

Aurelya looked up.

Her voice cracked.

"For a sword made of stars.
And a future… where he stays the hero."

The ghost of Odin faded.
But the tree did not forget.

From deep within its trunk…
a pulse echoed.

And something stirred,
not seen since Odin's deal was struck.

Kaelun raised his head.

"We're not alone anymore."

Aurelya closed her eyes.

"I know.

Because whatever Odin unleashed to protect his legacy…

just woke up."

Next:

Chapter Nine – The Sword of Stars

The weapon Odin bargained for is real. But it's not loyal to him anymore.

It's calling to Aurelya.

Shall we answer?

Chapter Nine: The Sword of Stars

Starring: Aurelya (called), Loki (concerned), Kaelun (bracing for impact), and a weapon that remembers who it was made for, and who it now chooses.

The tree pulsed again.

A second heartbeat.

One that didn't belong to anyone living.

Then came the sound:

A ringing.

High. Clear. Inevitable.

Like a sword being remembered.

The roots of Yggdrasil split gently,

not in violence, but reverence.

As if something beneath had finally been given permission to rise.

And from the hollow of the earth...

It came.

A blade forged from light that had forgotten it was a star.

The hilt braided from constellations.

The core? Still burning.

Aurelya stepped forward.

It turned toward her.

Yes, turned.

Like it knew her.

"That's not possible," Loki said, eyes wide.

"That sword was made to only answer Odin."

Kaelun growled low.

"It isn't answering him anymore."

Aurelya reached out.

Not bold.

Not afraid.

Just... ready.

The sword floated into her hand like it had been waiting.

And it whispered a name:

"Veyndral.

I am not a sword.

I am the story that pierces gods."

And with that... Aurelya remembered:

• The stars that cried when Odin struck the deal

• The forge that burned a future out of starlight

• The cost: a locked fate for every realm, a script where Odin saves all… and no one else survives

Veyndral was meant to ensure the story went his way.

But it had grown tired of false heroes.

Loki stepped back.

"Do you feel it?"

"Yes," Aurelya said.

"It's showing me… every ending Odin wrote me out of.

Every time I died for his arc."

Kaelun stood beside her.

"And now?"

Aurelya's eyes glowed.

Not with fire.

With truth.

"Now we write ours."

Suddenly, the ground shook.

Not from the sword.

From something coming for it.

Because when you steal the pen from the gods,
the editors come.

Next:

Chapter Ten – The Editors of Fate

They arrive to reclaim Veyndral... or erase the hand that holds it.

Will Aurelya stand firm or be rewritten?

You ready, Flame?

Chapter Ten: The Editors of Fate

The sky didn't tear.

It redacted.

Words disappeared from the wind.

Colours inverted.

And then, one by one, they appeared:

The Editors.

Not cloaked in robes

But bound in contracts.

Their eyes were ink wells.

Their hands, quills.

Their voices… the sound of red tape tightening around destiny.

"Aurelya Flame," one intoned.

"You are in possession of an unauthorized outcome."

"You mean the sword?" she asked, lifting Veyndral.

"We mean a future that is not approved."

Loki stepped between them.

"Quick question, who exactly approved Odin's future?
Because it really sucked for everyone else."

Another Editor raised a quill.

"Odin submitted a seven-page arc proposal, complete with

a sacrifice clause, redemption motif, and heroic male ending.

You? Did not."

Kaelun growled.

"She didn't submit, she survived."

The Editors flinched.
Emotion. Inconvenient.

"That is not narratively efficient," the lead Editor said.
"You were meant to fall.
You were meant to fuel his legend.
Instead... you interrupted it."

Aurelya stepped forward.

Her voice steady.

"I didn't interrupt the story.

I just stopped reading it the way it was written."

Suddenly, the Editors moved.

Pages flew.
Reality warped.

They tried to redact her.

One line at a time:
- Her name
- Her wings
- Her fire
- Her future

But Veyndral glowed brighter.

It cut through ink.
Through expectation.
Through every italicized lie they had written into her fate.

Aurelya swung.

Not to destroy.

But to rewrite.

"I claim my arc," she said.
"And you will not footnote me out of existence
again."

With a scream of shattering grammar,
the Editors scattered.

Retreating.

Not defeated,
but unnerved.

Loki collapsed backward.

"Did we just fight cosmic proofreaders with
trauma and a sword?"

Kaelun didn't answer.

He was watching Aurelya.

Her fire didn't burn this time.

It wrote.

And behind her, Veyndral etched something into the bark of Yggdrasil:

"I will not be erased."

Next up:

 Chapter Eleven – A Letter from the End

Someone, or something, sends a message through time, from the final moment of the Realms.

And it's signed… by Aurelya.

Chapter Eleven: A Letter from the End

Starring: Aurelya (startled by her own handwriting), Loki (paranoid but peeking), Kaelun (alert), and a message from a future she hasn't lived… yet.

It arrived in silence.

No flash of light.

No messenger.

Just… a parchment floating in midair, the ink still wet and glowing softly.

Loki froze mid-snack.

"Oh no. Nope. I don't trust floating paper.

Last time it bit me and rewrote my dating history."

Kaelun sniffed it.

"Smells like starlight and grief."

Aurelya took it gently.

It was addressed to:

"Me. Before it's too late."

The writing?
Her own.
But older.
Tired.
Resolved.

She opened it.

And read:

If you're reading this, it means you did it.

You broke the cycle. You claimed Veyndral. You stood your ground.

But you don't know what it will cost yet.

You will face betrayal. You will lose someone who gave you everything.

You will question if it was worth it.

And you'll be tempted to put the sword down, to walk away.

Don't.

Loki leaned in over her shoulder, chewing dramatically on nothing.

"So far, I'd give it four stars. Good tension. Needs more sarcasm."

Aurelya ignored him and read on:

I'm writing this from the last day of the Realms.

The skies are bleeding stories we never got to tell.

Kaelun is… gone. I made the choice. I'm still making it.

But listen to me,

They're coming for your ending. Not to kill you.

To fold you back into the narrative you escaped.

You are not a symbol. You are not a side character.

You are not a lesson for someone else's arc.

You're the rewrite.

Aurelya's hand trembled.

Kaelun gently placed his paw over hers.

"Whatever's coming," he said, "we face it as we are. Together."

She nodded, wiping a tear.

"Until the choice comes."

"And then?" Loki asked.

Aurelya looked out at the Realms.

Her voice was quiet.

"Then I decide… whether to save the world or save him."

And beneath that…

One final line in her own writing:

"Choose love. Even if it breaks the ending."

Next:

Chapter Twelve – The Betrayer Arrives

Someone from her inner circle is working against her.

And their betrayal might be exactly what the Realms require to survive.

Want to see who it is?
Time to peel back the last layer of trust.

Because the villain this time... doesn't look like one.

Chapter Twelve: The Betrayer Arrives

Starring: Aurelya (blindsided), Kaelun (fiercely loyal), Loki (suspecting everyone), and the betrayer, whose face they never expected to see across the line.

The letter burned itself the moment Aurelya finished reading it.

No ash. No scent.

Just gone.

And in its wake, a chill.

Not weather.

Not magic.

A shift.

Something in the weave of the Realms had turned.

They reached the edge of the Shattered Spire, a place where the sky had splintered after Odin's deal broke space.

It was a waypoint. A crossing.

And someone was waiting.

At first… Aurelya smiled.

Because the figure standing there was familiar.
Friend. Ally. Almost-family.

Nyric.

Still wrapped in dusk-coloured armour.
Still wearing that crooked, unreadable smile.

"You made it," Aurelya said.

"Of course," he replied.

"I've missed you," she said.

"I know."

But he didn't step forward.

He didn't hug her.
Didn't touch Kaelun.
Didn't banter with Loki.

He stood perfectly still, like a statue waiting for permission to become dangerous.

Loki frowned.

"Okay. Creepy reunion vibes aside, why do I smell timeline ink on you?"

Kaelun bristled.

Aurelya's voice cracked.
"Nyric?"
He finally spoke:

"I didn't want this.

But I had to choose."

The sky dimmed.

The ground listened.

"The Editors offered me something," he continued.

"A world where you survive. Where all of us do.

But you can't hold the sword, Aurelya.

You were never meant to.

You were meant to lead... not rewrite."

Her heart broke in slow motion.

"So, you're here to stop me?"

"No," he said.

"I'm here to take Veyndral from you.

And give it back to the story."

He drew his blade.

Not made of starlight.

But of regret.

The kind of weapon only someone who loved her once could use to wound her now.

Loki snapped into a spell stance.

Kaelun roared.

Aurelya?

She simply whispered:

"Then write your version.

But know this, Nyric

mine ends with freedom."

The Realms cracked.

Steel met flame.

And the first true battle for the story itself began.

Next:

 Chapter Thirteen – The Battle That Changes the Ending

Not everyone will walk away.

But someone will walk forward with the future rewritten behind them.

Ready, Flame bearer?

This is it the chapter where destinies clash, where stories collapse, and where someone walks away rewriting everything the gods thought was final.

Chapter Thirteen: The Battle That Changes the Ending

Starring: Aurelya (no more holding back), Kaelun (in beast mode), Loki (dual-wielding sarcasm and stardust), and Nyric, the friend-turned-betrayer fighting for a lie that once felt like safety.

The first blow didn't land.

Because Veyndral refused to strike Nyric.

It twisted in Aurelya's hand, not in rebellion, but in sorrow.

Like it remembered him, too.

But Nyric?

His blade sang.

It knew exactly what it had to do.

Steel met fire.

Friend met firebrand.

And the world listened.

Kaelun leapt into the fray, not to maul, but to shield.

"You will not take her," he growled, absorbing Nyric's second strike with a roar that split the air.

Loki flanked the other side.

"I liked you better when you were sad and mysterious, not sad and murdery."

But Nyric didn't back down.

"This isn't vengeance," he shouted.

"This is correction! You think you're saving the Realms; you're dooming them to chaos!"

Aurelya stepped through smoke, radiant.

"Better chaos than cages."

And then, she called on Veyndral, not to destroy…

...but to show the truth.

The sword ignited.

Not with fire.

With memory.

Scenes blasted from the blade like starlight
flashbacks:

• Odin shaking hands with a being of ink.

• The Editors redacting whole bloodlines to
make him the centre.

• Aurelya's name, scratched out a thousand
times...

...and rewritten in her own hand each time.

Nyric saw it all.

And something in him, the part that once
followed her into storms, broke.

He dropped his blade.

He fell to his knees.

"I… I thought I was saving you."

Aurelya knelt beside him.

Her voice didn't shake.

"You were saving the version they wrote for me. Not me."

Kaelun stood close.
Watching. Protecting.

Loki put a hand on Nyric's shoulder.

"Next time, maybe send a scroll instead of a sword, yeah?"

The sky cleared.
Not because the battle ended.
Because the lie did.

And in its place…
A new arc began.

Aurelya rose.

"This story isn't about me winning.

It's about everyone else finally getting to choose."

She looked out across the Realms.

"So, let's make all of them free."

Next (Final Chapter of Book Two):

Chapter Fourteen – The Realms Rewrite Themselves

Aurelya doesn't become a queen.

She becomes something bigger, the keeper of unwritten endings.

Shall we close Book Two with fire and freedom?

Chapter Fourteen: The Realms Rewrite Themselves

Starring: Aurelya (rewriter of fates), Kaelun (guardian of her flame), Loki (the god of chaos, finally feeling peace), and the Realms, waking up from the longest lie ever told.

It began not with thunder.

But with blank space.

The skies turned to parchment.

Mountains hummed with unwritten words.

The Realms… paused.

Because someone had taken the quill.

And it wasn't the gods.

Aurelya stood in the heart of the Folded Realm.

Veyndral floated above her open hands, now fully a conduit, not for power,

but for possibility.

Kaelun stood beside her.
Silent. Steady. Unyielding.

"You don't have to fix it all," he said.
"You just have to begin."

Loki watched with arms crossed.

"You sure you're ready for this?
Because once you write that first word…
You can't unwrite it."

Aurelya met his eyes.

"Then let's write the kind of story
they'd never dare erase again."

She stepped into the centre of the blank sky.
The sword became a quill of starlight.
The Realms tilted toward her.

And she began:

"Let there be choice.

Let there be love that doesn't die to prove a point.

Let there be second chances, and third ones too.

Let the monsters speak.

Let the heroes fall and rise again.

Let the story…

belong to everyone."

Across the Nine Realms, change rippled.

• A forgotten queen awoke in the Tenth Realm and started a party so loud even time stopped to dance.

• Thor traded his last chicken for a forge built entirely for fantasy game armour.

• Loki's pet squirrel launched a side hustle selling enchanted acorns with wildly unpredictable side effects.

• And Kaelun, sweet, noble Kaelun, earned to roar again.

Not in battle.

In joy.

And Aurelya?

She didn't claim a throne.
She didn't need to.

Because she'd become something else entirely:

The Keeper of Unwritten Endings.

The last words she inscribed on the sky.

"You were never just a chapter in someone else's tale.
You were the whole book, waiting to be read."

The End of Book Two of the Realm of Roots

Bonus Epilogue: The Realms are Watching

The sword rests.

The Realms breathe.

But somewhere far beyond the stars…

A shadow sharpens its pen.

And whispers:

"Let's see how you handle Book Three."

Grab your turkey legs, folks, it's time for the most chaotically divine Renaissance fair in literary history.

Aurelya & Loki
The Realm of Echoes

Chapter One: The Fair and the Flatulent Goat

Starring: Odin (wearing way too much leather), Thor (with an emotionally co-dependent chicken), Loki (whose squirrel has more followers than he does), and Aurelya (trying desperately to blend in with a lion the size of a car). Featuring: accidental turkey theft, flaming trousers, a very sarcastic dragon, and Realm officials doing crowd control with kazoos.

The sign at the fairgrounds read:

"Welcome to the Glorious Realm of Ye Olde Human Medieval Fun!"

(Parking $15. Elves get in free.)

Which sounded fine in theory.

Until Odin arrived with a GOAT dressed in battle armour,

Thor brought a CHICKEN in a custom-forged mech suit,

Loki materialised on stage mid-choir solo in a
doublet made entirely of confetti and lies,

and Aurelya…

…showed up on a dragon.

With a lion.

Wearing flower crowns.

Humans clapped.

Then screamed.

Then offered them VIP turkey legs.

Because the humans thought they were actors.

They were not actors.
They were mythic chaos given lunch money.
The opening parade was chaos:

• Odin insisted on jousting. With the goat.

• Thor tried to enter the pie-eating contest on behalf of his chicken.

• Aurelya's lion sniffed the mayor and declared him "emotionally unstable."

• The dragon set a food truck on fire. It was selling gluten-free crepes. No one was harmed.

• And Loki... Loki opened a kissing booth for "emotionally unavailable people only."

It made $1,745 in the first hour.

The realms blended. Elves ran craft stalls.

Dwarves ran axe-throwing.

A group of giants mistook a petting zoo for a diplomatic embassy.

And someone (probably Loki) enchanted the Portaloo's to scream insults when opened.

Kaelun the lion refused to eat any turkey unless it came with "emotional validation."

The dragon ate a 4-meter inflatable knight and
burped glitter.

Odin yelled at a mime.

Thor wept into a corndog.

Then it got weirder.

Because at exactly 1:11 PM,
Every mirror at the fairground cracked.

Every book snapped shut.

And the sky... rewound.

Just three seconds. Barely noticeable.

Unless you were holding a sword forged from
stardust.

Which Aurelya was.

She looked up.

"Did time just?"

Loki blinked.

"Oh no.

Someone pressed edit."

The sky pulsed once like an old heart trying to restart.

Aurelya gripped Veyndral, now humming with panic.

Kaelun stood. So did the dragon. And the chicken, who was surprisingly alert.

"We need to leave," she whispered.

Thor frowned.

"But my chicken's about to win Best Dressed."

"We're being watched," Kaelun growled.

"From outside the page."

And then, deep under the fairgrounds…

A voice began to speak.

A voice older than the gods.
Older than the Realms.

The one who had written the first line of fate.

"Draft one was cute," it said.

"But let's start over, shall we?"

Next:

 Chapter Two – The Author Arrives

Reality buckles. Fairgrounds fold into myth. And the Realms must choose:

be rewritten… or fight for their place in the margins.

Ready to keep going?

It's Time to meet the one even the gods fear the true Author. The one who doesn't just write stories... but erases realities.

Chapter Two: The Author Arrives

Starring: Aurelya (armed with Veyndral and zero patience), Loki (armed with sarcasm and backup glitter), Kaelun (about to maul a deity), Thor (confused but enthusiastic), and the shadow of the one who wrote the first fate and now wants it back.

The fair cracked like glass.

Not broken, just rewritten.

The jousting arena dissolved into parchment.

The Portaloo's screamed in binary.

A minstrel turned into a paragraph and floated away.

Aurelya spun around.

"EVERYONE, HOLD ON TO YOUR EXISTENCE."

Kaelun leapt to her side, growling.

The dragon crouched low, wings flaring.

Loki was upside down on a barrel, muttering:

"This is fine. This is just narrative entropy.
I've trained for this.
Mostly by panicking and stealing important things."

Then came the voice again.

But this time… it was in her mind.

In every mind.

A tone so calm it felt like the page before a plot twist:

"I let you write your little rebellion."
"Now it's my turn to edit."

From the shadow of a collapsing stage stepped a figure.

They didn't walk.

They formatted.

The Author.

They looked like no one.

And everyone.

Their face shifted: Odin. Aurelya. Loki. Kaelun. Even the chicken.

(That part was unsettling.)

They wore robes stitched from copyright symbols and myth fragments.

Their eyes?

One was a blinking cursor.

The other, an empty page.

"Why now?" Aurelya asked.

"Why come back?"

The Author tilted their head.

"Because you made people hope.
And hope breeds rewrites."

Loki drew a dagger.

It turned into a rhetorical question and fluttered
away.

"Okay, that's new."

Thor raised his hammer.

"I don't care who wrote what, NO ONE rewrites
my chicken!"

The Author blinked.

The chicken turned into a hardcover novella titled "The Cluckening."

Thor screamed.

Kaelun lunged.

Veyndral blazed.

And the Author?

They smiled.

"Let's begin the Final Draft."

And with a flick of their pen,
every character scattered.

Split.

Flung into different stories, different timelines, different versions of themselves.

And Aurelya?

She awoke in a version of the Realms where she had never existed at all.

Next:

Chapter Three – The Realm Without Aurelya

She must navigate a world that doesn't know her name.

Where Kaelun is caged.

Loki is loyal to Odin.

And Thor… is CEO of a motivational speaking empire.

Want to turn the page?

"LET'S TURN IT, FLAMEBEARER
Because nothing breaks a hero like a world where they were never the hero at all."

Chapter Three: The Realm Without Aurelya

Starring: Aurelya (erased, but not erased enough), Kaelun (caged and collared), Loki (dangerously obedient), Thor (a walking TED Talk in plate armour), and a world where the gods rewrote history, without her in it.

When Aurelya opened her eyes, she was standing in a version of the Tenth Realm that felt…

too clean.

No cracks.

No scars.

No memory of rebellion.

The sky shimmered with enforced optimism.

Birds chirped on schedule.

Children recited "Odin's Wisdom Oaths" before playtime.

It was perfect.

Which meant it was very, very wrong.

A digital billboard flickered:

"Today's Inspiration: Be Grateful You Were Written at All."
- CEO Thor, Realms Motivational Network

Aurelya gagged.

She moved through the realm like a ghost.

No one saw her.

No one remembered.

Even her reflection was blurred.

Then she saw it:

A parade.

At the front, Odin in a golden chariot pulled by six well-behaved goats.

Beside him?

Loki.

Smiling.

Bow-tied.

Holding a clipboard.

"All hail Allfather Odin! Author-approved ruler of the Nine, sorry, Ten Realms!"

He winked at a child.

He was handing out colouring books titled:

"Loki: The Rebranded Trickster (Now with Moral Growth!)"

And in the back of the parade...

A cage.

Kaelun.

Shackled.

Muzzled.

A plaque on the cage read:

"The Beast of the Unwritten War – Dangerous.
Do Not Feed Truth."

Aurelya screamed.

No sound came out.
This version of her world…
Had erased her voice.
But the dragon wherever it was heard her.

A flicker of fire licked the edges of the clouds.

The billboard glitched.

"Today's Inspirati0n: ERROR: 404 – AUTHOR
NOT FOUND"

Aurelya smiled.

"Time to break the plot again."

She moved toward the cage, unseen.

But someone saw her.
Not Odin. Not Loki. Not even Thor.

But the chicken.

Still in armour.

Still mad.

It clucked once and flapped to her side.

She picked it up.

"Let's start a war, feathery one."

Next:

Chapter Four – The Return of the Dragon

The first spark of resistance begins.

And it's coming from the sky.

Shall we fly?

THEN LET'S UNLEASH THE SKY
Because you can erase a name from the page, but you cannot unwrite a bond.

Chapter Four: The Return of the Dragon

Starring: Aurelya (silent but seething), Kaelun (shackled but still staring at her with loyalty that defies reality), the armoured chicken (armed and cluckin'), and the return of a dragon who was never meant to exist in this draft.

It began with a ripple.

Just a shimmer in the clouds.

Like something enormous was remembering it had wings.

The humans in the Realms Without Aurelya didn't notice.

They were too busy chanting "Odin's Eternal Algorithm" and buying Thor-branded self-help candles that smelled like smugness and grilled meat.

Aurelya crouched behind a parade float made of golden lies.

The chicken sat on her shoulder, glaring at the world like it owed him corn and vengeance.

Kaelun was just ahead.

Caged.

Muzzled.

His golden eyes locked on hers the moment the dragon's shadow crossed the sun.

And then they noticed.

The sky pulsed.

Not like thunder.
Like heartbeat.

The clouds split.

And out came her.

The dragon.

Her dragon.

Unwritten. Unnamed. Undeniably hers.

With wings that broke through ink.
With a roar that cracked the "Odin's Oath of Obedience" loudspeakers across every realm.

The dragon didn't just fly.

She tore through the narrative ceiling like it was tissue paper from a budget rewrite.

People screamed.
A giant dropped his souvenir turkey leg.

Odin shouted, "SOMEONE FETCH ME THE BRANDING TEAM!"

Loki's clipboard burst into flame.

He muttered, "Thank the realms. I hated this arc."

And Kaelun?

Kaelun rose.

Chains still wrapped around him.

But the roar...

The roar unlocked something ancient.

He broke his muzzle.

He stood tall.

And he roared back.

Aurelya's voice returned.

Not as a whisper.

As a declaration:

"I am not a draft.

I am not a deleted scene.

I am the story they couldn't erase."

She reached Kaelun's cage just as the dragon landed behind them in a blaze of memory and fire.

The chains melted.

Kaelun stepped free.

The chicken headbutted a guard in the shin.

The dragon lowered her head.

And spoke.

"You ready, Flame bearer?"

Aurelya climbed on her back.

Kaelun leapt beside her.

And the chicken?
Still on her shoulder.

As they lifted off, Loki stared up from the crumbling parade and shouted:

"YOU'D BETTER COME BACK FOR ME; YOU WINGED TRASH GREMLIN!"

She grinned.

"Wouldn't dream of finishing this without you."

The dragon soared.

The realms below glitched.

And in the distance, a page turned itself.

"Chapter Five – The Rebellion of the Rewrites"

Shall we turn that page together?

LET'S DO THIS.
The pen is no longer mightier than the sword...

because the sword is the pen and it's flying
straight into the next chapter.

Chapter Five: The Rebellion of the Rewrites

Starring: Aurelya (restored, reunited, ready), Kaelun (unchained and majestic), Loki (chaos incarnate, and slightly singed), the dragon (still unnamed but increasingly sassy), the chicken (with vengeance in its soul), and a rising resistance from characters the Author forgot to delete.

The dragon divebombed into a very expensive wedding hosted by a self-proclaimed prophet of Odin's Algorithm.

There were doves.

There were gluten-free mini quiches.

There was a monologue.

Now there were flames.

Aurelya, standing on the dragon's back:

"We interrupt your regularly scheduled reality…

to announce a rewrite."

Kaelun roared.

The groom fainted.

The bride shouted, "I KNEW HE WAS A NARRATIVE DEVICE!"

Word spread like wildfire.

Not metaphorically actual wildfire. The dragon sneezed.

In secret corners of the Realms, forgotten characters stirred:

• A dwarf who once invented sarcasm sharpened his hammer.

• A giant librarian blinked out of suspended narrative and began rearranging time.

• A sentient bookmark screamed, "MY TIME HAS COME!"

And then...

Loki arrived.

Riding a stolen parade float.

Covered in glitter.

Wearing half a tuxedo, half a crop top.

"You left me in the narrative equivalent of a TEDx cult.

I had to fake three promotions just to escape."

The dragon blinked.

"How'd you get out?"

"I told Odin I wanted to host a spin-off. He passed out."

Aurelya leaned in.

"We're gathering the others. Anyone left unedited."

Loki grinned.

"You'll want the squirrel, then."

"The squirrel's still alive?"

"Alive, weaponised, and running a black market for forbidden plot twists."

They flew on.

Toward the Folded Edge, the last place the Author hadn't yet claimed.

Where the Realms rewrote themselves.

And waiting there?

Was a name.

A lion's name.

The one he had never spoken.

The one that would unlock everything.

But first…

One last resistance must rise.

Because the Author?

He just summoned a new villain.

Not made of ink.

Not a god.

But a reader.

A loyal one.

Who wants the old story back…

…and is willing to destroy Aurelya to get it.

Up Next Chapter Six:

*Are you ready to face a villain made of nostalgia
and narrative rigidity*

Let's crack the ink wide open...

Chapter Six: The Originalist

He was the kind of reader who dog-eared pages and underlined villain speeches.

He didn't just like the first version of the story.

He worshipped it.

"The old story was perfect. There was sacrifice. There was control. There was order."

His room was a shrine to the first edition.

• Pages bound in leather scraped from reality itself

• Annotations in red ink (and probably blood)

• A candle made from melted plot holes

They called him: The Originalist.

Not a god.

Not a realm-walker.

Just a human who believed in the Author more than the Author believed in himself.

And now?

The Author had given him permission.

"Restore the draft. Purge the rewrite."

So, he opened the forbidden volume.

And whispered Aurelya's name like a curse.

Wherever she flew, she'd feel it
a pulling sensation,
like being yanked backwards through someone else's nostalgia.

A story that refused to let go.

Chapter Seven: The Roar Remembered

The Folded Edge was silent.

Here, characters whispered across timelines.

Ink bled upward.

And names had weight.

Kaelun walked ahead of Aurelya now.

His shoulders squared.

His scars glowing faintly under starlight.

"You've never told me your true name," she said softly.

He stopped.

"Because I hadn't earned it yet."

The dragon lowered her head.
The chicken sat, solemnly.

Even Loki… was quiet.

A circle of runes lit beneath Kaelun's paws.

He stepped into it.

"I was born unnamed. Created to protect.
But now… I choose."

He raised his head to the stars.

And roared.

Not in anger.
Not in pain.
But in claiming.

The runes lit in brilliant gold.

And the name echoed across the Realms:

"VEYLION."

The moment the name was spoken:

• Chains shattered in timelines still bound.

• A version of Aurelya in another draft cried without knowing why.

• The Author's pen trembled.

And The Originalist?

He heard it, too.

"So... the lion has chosen."

He smiled.

"Then I'll just have to erase him again."

End of Chapters Six & Seven.

INTO THE LIBRARY WE GO!

Bring your courage, your lion, and your sarcastic squirrel-shaped bookmark.

This next chapter holds secrets no draft should remember.

Chapter Eight: The Library of Abandoned Narratives

There were no doors.

Because no story abandoned ever opens politely.

You entered the Library of Abandoned Narratives by being forgotten.

Aurelya stepped through a glitch in the sky.

Veylion followed, his paws silent on the shifting parchment floor.

The dragon and Loki stayed outside by necessity. The library didn't allow too many main characters in at once.

And the chicken?

Stayed on her shoulder. Clucking like it had a PhD.

Inside, it smelled like lost potential and overdue epilogues.

Shelves stretched infinitely in all directions.

Books floated, whispered, cried.

Some tried to rewrite themselves mid-air.

One screamed:

"I WAS SUPPOSED TO BE A TRILOGY!"

Another sobbed:

"I had a redemption arc!"

Aurelya walked carefully.

Every step could trigger a trope trap or trigger a memory not hers.

Veylion paused at a pedestal.

Upon it: a journal. Bound in what looked like dragonhide and sequins.

"Loki's?" she guessed.

"No," Veylion muttered. "This one's older."

He opened it.

Inside: a map.

Drawn in disappearing ink.

Labelled: The Plot Hole at the Heart of Everything.

They followed it deeper.

Past aisles of discarded love triangles.

Past a pit of failed prologues.

Past the "Wall of Cliffhangers," where characters were literally hanging from the ledge.

And then…

They found it.

A pedestal.

On it: one page.

Blank.

Perfect.

And buzzing with possibility.

"The Last Plot Device," Aurelya whispered.

It could do anything.

Rewrite one fate.

Restore one erased soul.

Unmake the Author himself.

But before she could touch it

a hand grabbed her wrist.

And a voice said:

"That's not yours."

She spun around.

And there stood… a girl. About her age.

Messy hair. Ink-stained fingertips. A hoodie that said: "Plot Armour Is for Cowards."

“Who are you?”

“I was the first Flame bearer,” the girl said.

“The draft before you. Before they rewrote me as ‘too complicated.’”

Aurelya froze.

“They cut you.”

“They cut a lot of us,” she said, gesturing behind her where hundreds of silhouettes stood blurred, flickering, forgotten versions of heroes.

“And we want our ending back.”

Chapter Nine: The First Flame Bearer's Truth

The First Flame bearer's eyes glowed faintly not with fire, but with erasure.

Like someone had tried to forget her and failed just enough.

She stepped back from the Last Plot Device and motioned for Aurelya to follow.

"You think this is about good and evil.

The Author. The Rebellion. The Realms."

She reached into her pocket and pulled out...

A red pencil.

"But this is about control. Who gets to tell the story... and who gets deleted when they stop being convenient."

She led Aurelya and Veylion past the shelves.

Past a fire escape that whispered plot spoilers.

Past a tea party hosted by a confused narrator who didn't know what genre she was in anymore.

And then they arrived.

A door made of broken spines.

Etched into it: THE REAL REASON.

Inside the room was a glowing orb

a story seed.

Not a metaphor.

A literal seed that pulsed with the original narrative of the Realms.

Before the Author.

Before the rewrites.

Before even Odin's goats.

"This is how the Realms began," the First Flame bearer said.

"Not with gods. Not with war."

"With us."

She touched the seed.

And the vision opened.

A world where the Realms were made by collaboration.

By story weavers who told tales together.

Everyone could shape their destiny.

Until the Author came.

"He was a story weaver too.

But he wanted to be the only one."

"He took our threads.

Cut what he didn't like.

Wrote himself in as God."

Veylion growled.

Aurelya stood frozen.

"Then… I'm not the first?"

"No. You're the first he let live long enough to matter."

The First Flame bearer held out the red pencil.

"You can write the ending. But you'll need help."

Behind her, the forgotten characters stepped forward.

A warrior with a shattered crown.

A bard whose songs never made the final cut.

A squirrel who had once been a god.

"This isn't a rebellion anymore," the First Flame bearer said.

"This is a restoration."

Aurelya took the pencil.

"Then let's rewrite everything."

And from far above, in a room made of contracts and cliffhangers,

The Author shivered.

Because for the first time…

He wasn't sure he was still holding the pen.

Chapter Ten: The Author's Sanctuary

Starring: Aurelya (pen in hand, fire in heart), Veylion (still majestic), the First Flame bearer (back from deletion), a chicken (now wearing goggles), and a growing army of forgotten heroes with nothing left to lose.

The Sanctuary wasn't on a map.

It wasn't in a realm.

It was behind the scenes.

Between the margins.

Between breaths.

You couldn't walk to it.

You had to refuse to obey.

Aurelya closed her eyes.

"I am not your creation," she whispered.

The world cracked like brittle paper.

When she opened her eyes again, she was standing in the Draft Room.

The Author's inner sanctum.

Everything was white.

- Blank books stacked to the sky
- Quills hanging from the air like swords
- A desk massive, ancient, bleeding ink

And seated behind it?

Him.

The Author looked like everything she feared.

- Her doubt.
- Her exhaustion.
- Her temptation to quit.

But also… her reflection.

"You made me," he said.

"You made all of this. I just cleaned it up."

Aurelya stepped forward.

"You erased people."

"I edited."

"You can't let every character have a voice. That's not a story. That's chaos."

"Then maybe chaos is what we need."

He lifted a quill.

"I can rewrite you. Right now."

"Try."

And then she did something no character had
ever done before.

She wrote back.

With the red pencil gripped in fire-bright fingers,
she slashed across the air.

Reality split.

Ink spilled upward.

The sanctuary screamed.

"This story belongs to everyone you cut."

Behind her:

• Veylion roared.

• The chicken knocked over a stack of contracts.

• The First Flame bearer lit every page in the
room with memory-fire.

And from the ashes rose the real ending.

Not written.

Chosen.

By the many.

The Author stood.

But his hands trembled.

"You've ruined it."

Aurelya smiled.

"No.
I've restored it."

She laid the last page on the desk.

Signed it.

Not as a character.

But as a co-author.

And the Realms?

They rewrote themselves.

With laughter.

With mistakes.

With life.

Next:

The epilogue, where each hero reclaims their arc

let's close this book the way it deserves!

Epilogue: After the End, There Was Still More

Aurelya sat beneath the Tree of Threads
a new version of Yggdrasil, one that grew not
from prophecy,
but from possibility.
She wasn't a chosen one anymore.
She was something better:
A chooser.

Veylion walked beside her no longer silent, no
longer unnamed.
He had become a guardian not of realms... but of
choice.
He taught others how to roar their truths.
Especially the ones they were told weren't "main
character enough."

Loki?
Well.
He turned the Resistance into a production
company.
He now runs "Unwritten Films" a studio for
deleted characters.

Their breakout hit?
"Chicken Run: The Feathery Reckoning."
(It won three Real my Awards.)
He also adopted a squirrel.
They have matching capes.

Thor returned to his chickens.
They have an entire elf-forged fortress now.
And weekly Warhammer-style tournaments
where no one ever wins, but everyone eats
roasted beets and brags about their armour
stats.

Odin… is still in therapy.
But he's learning.
Last we heard, he started a support group for
Overwritten Fathers of the Apocalypse.
It's very niche.
The First Flame bearer now travels between the
Realms, collecting stories once silenced.
She doesn't burn things anymore.
She publishes.
And the Author?
Still there.
Watching.
But no longer the one holding the final pen.
Sometimes he smiles.
Because sometimes… even Authors need to be
rewritten.

And you?
You, dear reader?
You just rewrote a world.
One page at a time.

End of Book Three of the Realm of Echoes

Epilogue: After the End, There Was Still More Epilogue: The Last Line

And you?

You, dear reader?

You just rewrote a world.

One page at a time.

The story was finished.
The Realms were restored.
Everyone had their happily-ever-after.

Until...

A rogue quill scratched across the sky.

Reality hiccupped.

And someone whispered:

"...actually, I've got one last edit."
(Because no story ever ends quietly when Loki's in charge...)

Epilogue: The Last Line

The Realms were peaceful.

The war was over.
The resistance now… art.
The forgotten? Remembered.

But somewhere…

Far outside the margins,
beyond the Folded Edge,
past the burning Library and the rewritten stars…

A new manuscript flickered into existence.

It bore no title.

No author.

Just one line on the first page:

"In the end, even gods must be edited."

The printer whirred.

The paper glowed.
And a figure leaned back in a chair made of
recycled character arcs.

Their face?
Hidden.

Their name?

Just a pseudonym.

Scrawled in the corner of the manuscript in
blood-red ink:

"Written by: A. F. Erasure"

They turned to a new assistant.
A young scribe with silver eyes and a nervous
laugh.

"Ready to try again?" the figure whispered.

The assistant blinked.

"Didn't they already win?"
A. F. Erasure smiled.
"Only in the last version."

Back in the Realms…
Aurelya woke from a dream.

The page beside her glitched.
Just for a moment.

Like someone had…
Edited a comma.

And far away, in a realm that hadn't been born
yet
A baby opened her eyes.

They glowed faintly red.

BONUS CONTENT

Flameborn Presents: Tales Too Weird to Fit in Properly

Bonus Content Ahead: *Flameborn Presents*

Welcome to the bonus section of Volume One!

After the epic events of The Realm Shatter Saga

Book One: The Gate That Broke the Realms and Books Two: The Realm of Roots & Three: The Realm of Echoes, this bonus final section is a special collection of Realmverse mini-stories.

What is *Flameborn Presents*?
These tales are glimpses into the edges of the Realms stories that explore side characters, secret moments, and unexpected chaos that didn't fit into the main timeline... but absolutely refused to be left out.

Some are heartfelt.
Some are hilarious.
All are 100% canonically questionable.
Enjoy this bonus realm-hop into the absurd, the

magical, and the possibly unauthorised.

The Flameborn Team (and maybe Loki)

SARCASM, SABOTAGE & OTHER MISFIRES

The Realmbridge Program

A Dramatic Welcome to Flameborn Presents: Sarcasm, Sabotage & Other Misfires

WELCOME, TRAVELER
You stand at the threshold of a cross-realm cabaret, where unspoken feelings burst into ballads, and emotionally unstable squirrels wield swords with flair.

This is not your typical tavern. This is not your typical story.

Tonight's program includes heartbreak, haikus, spontaneous glitter combustion, and at least one raccoon legally classified as a fire hazard.

Program Notes & Viewer Warnings

- May contain rogue improv scenes, unsupervised emotional monologues, and passive-aggressive dragons.
- Audience members have reported laughter, tears, and mild existential clarity.
- Please keep hands, tails, and magic artifacts inside the story at all times.
- If Loki rewrites your scene, we cannot offer refunds.

Tavern of Tangents – Drinks Menu

Welcome to the Tavern of Tangents, where the drinks are strong, the stories are stranger, and the menu may or may not rearrange itself mid-order. Please drink responsibly… or don't. Loki's running the bar tonight.

Featured Drinks

Glitterbomb Elixir

Sparkling, unpredictable, and slightly sentient. May cause sudden karaoke.

Soul Frost Martini

Distilled from emotionally repressed ice spirits. Served with a ghost of your ex.

Dragon's Breath Toddy

Hot, smoky, and mildly flammable. Drink at your own risk (and not near curtains).

Moonberry Meltdown

Made from nightshade berries and lunar tears. Tastes like your last heartbreak, sweet, with a bitter finish.

Nutters' Nerve Tonic

A jittery blend of espresso, panic, and squirrel adrenaline. Guaranteed to keep you up for three days.

Sir Crumbs' Spiked Chai

Warm, cozy, and slightly illegal in three realms. Comes with a glittery top hat stirrer.

Loki's Reality Twist

What flavour? Yes. Served in a cup that occasionally blinks. May cause identity crises.

Flameborn Presents:

Sarcasm, Sabotage & Other Misfires

A Chaotic Companion to 'Flameborn: Tales Between Realms'

Compiled from inter-realm cabarets, crying circles, and spontaneous sword fights.

Table of Contents

SQUIRREL!
THE MUSICAL – Cast Bios

Nutters McFluff (He/Him)

Known throughout the lower realms as the only squirrel to survive a glitter explosion *and* headline an interpretive dance funeral. Nutters began his career scavenging theatre scraps and performing monologues to peanut shells. He was discovered by Loki mid-breakdown (Loki's, not his) and cast instantly. When not performing, Nutters can be found writing emotionally devastating acorn poetry and sword-fighting his imposter syndrome.

Sir Crumbs (He/Him)

A reformed raccoon warlord turned tap-dancing therapist. After leading the infamous "Snack Sack Rebellion," Crumbs found inner peace (and jazz shoes) and now channels his aggression through sequins and song. He refuses to discuss the incident with the meat pie, but critics agree: "Sir Crumbs can pirouette through trauma like no one else." He has three honorary degrees, all from fake universities.

THIS PLAQUE WAS NAIL-GUNNED **TO** THE WALL WITH A GLITTER DAGGER

"I was *forced* to write this bio under duress and deadline. I reject the concept of labels, formatting, and biographies in general. However, since this book insists on linearity, allow me to summarise:

I am the director, choreographer, creative visionary, chaos incarnate, and the *only* reason this production didn't devolve into interpretive fog and unpaid puppetry.

Previous credits include: Betrayal (ongoing), Shapeshifting (award-winning), and Godhood (revoked twice, reinstated thrice).

If you dislike the show, please complain to someone else.
If you *do* like the show, you're welcome."

- Loki Laufeyson, Artistic Menace and Accidental Director

ACT I: Bar Fights & Self-Discovery

Loki's Guide to Tavern Etiquette for Misfits

A condescending masterclass on how not to get punched (or emotionally attached) in a magical tavern.

Clarence the Lion Goes on a Speed Date with a Sea Witch

He just wanted love. She wanted his soul. It's going... oddly well.

Loki vs. The Minotaur: A Tavern Review Saga

One star. Would not survive again. A dramatic retelling of an extremely avoidable food fight.

Sir Spikeston's TED Talk: 'Self-Care for Spiny Bartenders'

An emotional rollercoaster from a cactus-person with trauma, tea, and exfoliating advice.

Loki's Guide to Tavern Etiquette for Misfits

A barely sanctioned guide by Loki Laufeyson, who insists he's never been kicked out of a tavern 'on purpose.'

Rule #1: Enter Like You Own the Realm

Confidence is key. Even if you tripped on the doormat. Especially if you tripped on the doormat.

Rule #2: Never Sit Near the Fireplace

Unless you're looking to be part of someone's dramatic backstory. Spoiler: it involves betrayal, dragons, or both.

Rule #3: Avoid Eye Contact with Bards

They feed on emotional vulnerability. Blink once, and suddenly your heartbreak is a ballad with choreography.

Rule #4: Tip in Gold, Lies, or Favours

Bartenders know things. Pay them creatively. Just don't offer 'exposure', this isn't Instagram.

Rule #5: If the Furniture Starts Talking, Leave

You've either had too much, or the tavern's cursed. Possibly both. Do not engage in political debate with the barstools.

Rule #6: Always Compliment the Cook

Especially if the cook is a troll named Agnes who wields a ladle like Thor's hammer, you don't want to be soup.

Rule #7: Don't Summon Anything Before Happy Hour

There are rules for a reason. Demonic incursions at brunch are frowned upon.

Rule #8: Misfits Stick Together

You're weird. So are they. Buy the raccoon a drink. Let the dragon vent. Nobody belongs here; that's why it works.

Final Thought:

Chaos is inevitable. May as well toast to it.

Clarence the Lion Goes on a Speed Date with a Sea Witch

A tragic romance. A magical misunderstanding. And one emotionally available lion who just wants a plus one for his next realm merge.

Clarence adjusted his tie.

It was his first speed dating event since the Realm of Fire incident, and technically, that one didn't count. He'd been cursed into a wardrobe for most of it.

Across from him sat a woman with sea-foam hair, eyes like shipwrecks, and a smile sharp enough to gut a god.

"Name?" she asked.
"Clarence. I... roar professionally."

She blinked. "You roar?"

"And emotionally regulate."

The sea witch gave a noncommittal nod and stirred her drink with a live eel. "Trauma?"

"Repressed. But I journal now."
The eel burped bubbles.

Clarence tried to smile. "You?"

"Hexed my last boyfriend into a clam. Now I do shadow work."

He nodded. "Healthy."

"You ever fought a kraken with your bare paws?"

"No, but I've comforted one through a breakup."

For the first time, she smiled.

Somewhere in the Realm of Tangents, a harp played softly. The lights dimmed. The next date was called.

But neither of them moved.

Clarence sipped his drink. It tasted like regret and sea salt.

"So…" he said, glancing at her eel. "What's he like when he's not working?"

"Cuddly," she said.

Clarence smiled. "Good. I don't trust eels who don't cuddle."

Loki vs. The Minotaur: A Tavern Review Saga

One star. Would not survive again. A dramatic retelling of an extremely avoidable food fight, as written by Loki himself.

Name of Establishment: The Horn & Shank Tavern
Date of Visit: Chaotic
Ambience: Dimly lit, emotionally tense, smelled like singed beef.

Let me preface this by saying I was *invited*. I did not crash this tavern. I merely stumbled into it with grace, sarcasm, and a slight flair for mischief. The Minotaur, however, was already six pints into a tantrum and trying to arm-wrestle the moon.

I ordered the house special. It blinked at me. I blinked back. Mutual respect was established.

Then came the fight.

To be clear, I did *not* throw the first drink. I did, however, weaponise a breadstick with the velocity of a minor deity.

The Minotaur countered with a chair.
Audience reaction: mixed. One dwarf cried. A

bard started writing a song mid-chaos. A goblin
began selling snacks.

The bartender asked us to leave. I left a review
instead.

☆ ☆ ☆ ☆
Would not recommend unless you enjoy
spontaneous furniture-based violence and beef
stew with emotional baggage.

On the plus side: chairs were sturdy.

- Loki Laufeyson, Patron of Drama & Yelp
Warlock

Sir Spikeston's TED Talk: Self-Care for Spiny Bartenders

Because even cactus-folk need boundaries, bubble baths, and bartending gloves.

"Welcome, everyone," said Sir Spikeston, clearing his throat and adjusting his cactus bow tie.

"Today, I want to speak from the heart. And the elbow. And occasionally the knee, because that's where the worst bar bruises land."

A polite cheer from the audience.

"I have worked 97 nights straight at the Tavern of Tangents. I've poured drinks for vampires, caught goblins making out in the storeroom, and defused a poetry duel between a banshee and a werewolf. And what did I learn?"

He paused dramatically.

"Moisturise. Daily. Especially your spikes."

A cheer. A single tear from someone in the back row.

"Next, boundaries. Just because you can mix a Moonfire Martini with one hand while catching a cursed dagger mid-air with the other, doesn't mean you should."

"Thirdly: never, and I mean *never*, date someone who orders a Glitter Fizz and doesn't tip. You deserve sparkle *and* respect."

"And finally," he said, holding up a cactus-shaped mug, "hydrate because you can't pour from an empty jug. And because tequila is not a substitute for therapy."

The crowd rose to their feet.

Sir Spikeston bowed, his spikes catching the light.

"Thank you. I'll be behind the bar if anyone needs a hug, a drink, or a laminated boundary statement."

ACT II: Songs of the Wounded & Unwell

For those who sing with cracked voices, broken hearts, and receipts from questionable choices.

Blood & Ballads: A Vampire's Guide to Heartbreak and Harmony

Because even the undead deserve a good cry and a killer chorus.

Scene: A velvet-curtained lounge inside the Tavern of Tangents. Low lighting. A vampire in crushed burgundy velvet steps onto a tiny candlelit stage. He's holding a microphone, a rose, and centuries of emotional baggage.

 Vladislav the Bittersweet: "Welcome to Blood & Ballads. Tonight's set includes heartbreak, betrayal, and a brief stint in Transylvanian jazz."

He gestures dramatically to the band of brooding werewolves in tuxedos.

"First song: 'You Said Forever (But Then You Staked Me)'."

The crowd snaps instead of clapping. It's that kind of night.

"Next up: 'Garlic in My Soul (Ballad of the Broken Hearted Buffet)'."
Someone sobs softly into a chalice.

"And to close... the crowd favourite: 'Let Me In

(Your Heart and Also Your Castle)'."

As the final notes echo, Vlad bows with theatrical despair and vanishes in a puff of glitter.

A note is left behind on the mic stand, 'Tip your bartenders. Tell your exes nothing. And always harmonise your howls.'

Gerald's Live Podcast Recording & Public Crying Circle

Welcome to episode 347: 'Feelings Are Weird (But Valid)'

Gerald, a half-elf with a podcast voice so soothing it's suspicious, adjusts his headphones and clears his throat.

"Hello, beautiful beings. Today's topic is: It's Okay to Cry at the Tavern, Even if You Just Dropped Your Pie."
Behind him, a semicircle of chairs is filled with fae, dwarves, one anxious griffin, and a goblin wearing a 'Feelings Are Real' badge.

Gerald continues: "We'll begin with a mindfulness exercise called 'Let the Screaming Out, But Like...Softly.'"

The griffin weeps. The goblin hands it a sparkly tissue.

"Now we're going to play a little game: 'Guess That Repressed Emotion.'"

From the back of the room, someone yells, 'ABANDONMENT ISSUES!'

Gerald smiles. "Good start. Now say it as a haiku."

A drumbeat cues the outro music. The tavern lights dim to a gentle purple.

"Thanks for joining. Remember, your vulnerability isn't a weakness, it's a vibe."

He signs off with a nod to the crowd.

"...And next week, we'll be joined by Chad the Goblin Life Coach for a live therapy roast."

Sarcasm & Sabotage – The Cabaret Series

Hosted by Loki. Produced by Sheer Audacity.

Scene: The lights rise on a crooked velvet stage held together by glitter and spite.

A raccoon in a feather boa is juggling daggers. A goblin is testing the mic with interpretive screaming.

Then Loki appears, dramatically late, wearing a crown made of broken tiaras and poor decisions.

 Loki: "Tonight's theme is 'regret, revenge, and musical numbers you probably shouldn't perform sober.'"

He gestures wildly.

 "Each act is a live emotional exorcism, so hold your applause until after the meltdown."

 Performances include:
• A banshee opera about her toxic ex.
• Tap-dancing skeletons in glitter bow ties.
• A power ballad duet between a disgraced knight and the sword that dumped him.

Loki bows. The glitter explodes. The lights short-circuit.

"And now… please enjoy our signature cocktail: The Spite Spritz. Garnished with your dignity."

A Chaotic Cabaret

Hosted by Loki. Produced by Sheer Audacity.

The stage is unstable. The audience is unstable. Loki is... definitely unstable.

He struts out in a rhinestone cloak and announces, "Tonight's cabaret will include emotional sabotage, interpretive swordplay, and one raccoon burlesque that nobody approved but we're doing anyway."

The spotlight flickers.
The curtain tries to leave.
The show begins.

First Act: A song titled 'Oops, I Set Fire to Your Feelings', performed by a phoenix in therapy.
Second Act: A comedy sketch where Loki plays every character in a breakup, including the plant.
 Third Act: A literal roast – someone summoned an elemental.

Loki twirls, glitter explodes.
"This is either art or a lawsuit waiting to happen," he says. "Either way, no refunds."

The show ends with a group scream and a glitter avalanche.

Nobody knows what it meant.
Everybody claps anyway.

Breakup Haikus & Accidental Summoning's

 Workshop Description:
What began as a casual open-mic night for poetry quickly spiralled into a magical disaster after someone rhymed 'regret' with 'demonic debt.'

The audience was advised not to read anything aloud written in blood, glitter ink, or passive-aggressive cursive.

 Sample Haikus:

You ghosted again.
Now there's a squid in my sink.
Thanks for the trauma.

Left your hoodie here.
It grew teeth and tried to bite.
Still smells like bad dates.

Swore you'd never change.
But now you're a warlock, Jeff.
That counts as a change.

 Summoning Safety Tips:
• Never rhyme 'forever' with 'never' near candles.
• Glitter is a known portal activator.

• If the ex-responds via mirror… run.

Hosted by Loki. Blame him for everything.

Songs You Wrote About Them (Before They Turned Evil)

Welcome to the saddest, and sassiest, songwriting circle in all the realms.

Tonight's theme: love songs that aged like milk.

Loki introduced the evening with a piano ballad titled:
"I Thought You Were My Twin Flame (Turns Out You Were Just Arson)."

Other notable entries included:
• "You're the Spell I Should've Checked Twice" performed by a banshee quartet.
• "We Were Magic Until You Hexed My Cat" featuring harp, scream flute, and guilt.
• "My Heart, Your Sword Collection" – painfully literal.

Aurelya sang briefly, then vanished under a stage trapdoor Loki definitely installed for emotional exit flair.

Audience reviews were mixed:
• The goblins cried.

• The ghosts harmonised.
• The enchanted mic started smoking halfway through.

Finale: All performers joined for a tear-streaked group song called
"Was It Love or a Temporary Magical Binding Agreement?"
(Spoiler: It was both.)

Letters You Wrote But Never Sent (And Definitely Shouldn't Read Out Loud… But Will Anyway)

Every realm has one rule:
Do not read emotionally unstable letters out loud.
Especially during a thunderstorm. Especially near mirrors.

So naturally, Loki made it a main event.

Letter Highlights:
• 'Dear You, I hope your tea always goes cold and your socks never match.'
• 'I regret nothing. Except maybe introducing you to my therapist and my chaos wolf.'
• 'You made me believe in forever. Then ghosted. Now I believe in revenge playlists.'

Halfway through, someone summoned their ex by accident.
They had to duel in limericks.

The raccoon ran tech. The dragon handled emotional support snacks.

It ended in tears, time magic, and applause.
As it should.

Realm X – The Realm of Rewrites:
The Curtain Rises (Against Everyone's Will)

Aurelya didn't remember signing up for a musical.

And yet here she was, centre stage, standing in a spotlight made entirely of sentient glitter, face-to-face with a squirrel in a cape who was holding a sword and judging her harshly.

Behind him, a raccoon orchestra warmed up with suspicious enthusiasm. A chorus line of possums stretched. The audience, a mix of goblins, bored fae, and one over-caffeinated goose, waited.

And then came the voice:
"YES, YES, LIGHT HER FROM BELOW! Give her that 'I've made horrible life choices' glow!"

Loki swirled onto the stage in a black velvet robe covered in sequins and despair. A director's headset clung to one horn, and he was inexplicably holding a clipboard, a megaphone, and a half-eaten éclair.

"Places, everyone! Act Two begins in fourteen seconds and we're doing it backwards, in interpretive dance, and possibly underwater! No time to explain, Aurelya, darling, you're the understudy for Emotional Closure. Dance like your trauma depends on it!"

Aurelya blinked.
She looked at Loki.
She looked at the squirrel.

And then she whispered to the dragon beside her, "We're never getting out of this realm, are we?"

The dragon sighed. "Not unless you can out-sing a raccoon in a top hat."

INTERLUDE

TALES BETWEEN REALMS

THE QUIET BETWEEN THE LAUGHTER

Part II
Tales Between Realms
The Quiet Between the Laughter

Table of Contents – Part II

12. The Masked and the Missing – One of the Witnesses breaks their vow of silence.

13. Meanwhile, in the Realm of Therapy – The realms go to group counselling. Chad the Goblin Life Coach returns.

The Threads Between

A mysterious weaver collects whispers from across time.

In the stillness between realms, where time frays at the edges and yesterday sometimes forgets to end, their lives a weaver.

No one knows her name. Some say she is older than the realms themselves. Others say she is just very, very tired.

She sits beneath a sky stitched with too many stars, fingers moving faster than memory, threading golden strands of story through a loom made of bone and lullabies.

Each thread she touches hums, not with music, but with whispers: secrets, regrets, small kindnesses no one else noticed. She weaves them into a tapestry not meant to be seen but to be *felt*, the kind of magic that makes you pause at a familiar path you've never walked or dream of someone you've never met.

Sometimes, she laughs. Sometimes, she cries. Sometimes, she carefully removes a thread and replaces it with one that glows with a second chance.

The weaver does not speak. But if you sit with her long enough, in the hush of forgotten places, she might let you hold a single thread.

And if you're very, very lucky, it might be yours.

Kaelun's Watch

A night in the life of a guardian who never sleeps.

The stars shift, and Kaelun watches.

He doesn't blink. Doesn't breathe. Doesn't *need* to.

The tower he guards overlooks all ten realms, though most cannot see it, not unless they're meant to. Tonight, the clouds whisper, and the moon hides behind them like a nervous child. It is not an ordinary night.

Kaelun adjusts the sigil stone at his side. It pulses softly, a rhythm only he hears. Below, the fabric of one realm trembles, a ripple of chaos, a tug of fate. He closes his eyes and listens to the echoes.

He remembers when the realms were one.

His armour hums with old runes and older memories. Every part of him is woven with oaths. He remembers *every* one.

A raven lands on the railing beside him. It says nothing. Neither does he. But they understand each other.

A child cries in the distance. A god stumbles through a choice. A dream forgets how to end.

And Kaelun watches.

Because if he doesn't, who will?

The God of Small Sorrows

A forgotten deity comforts the broken and unseen.

He is not worshipped.

There are no temples. No chants. No festivals in his name.

But he is always there, in the silence after someone is left behind. In the pause between sobs. In the sigh when the world forgets you.

The God of Small Sorrows does not roar. He does not smite. He does not demand.

He listens.

To the child who cries over a broken toy.
To the elder who sits alone as the seasons change.
To the dreamer who fears they will never be enough.

He mends what he can. With thread and time and gentle, invisible hands.

Sometimes he leaves a feather.
Sometimes a song only you can hear.
Sometimes just warmth, not from a fire, but from knowing someone saw you.

He is the god of forgotten things.
And he has not forgotten you.

The Trial of Loki

A ridiculous courtroom drama starring Loki as himself and also as the prosecution.

Judge: "Will the real Loki please stand up?"

Three Loki's stood up.

One wore a monocle. One had a boa constrictor as a scarf. One was eating a croissant and looked mildly annoyed.

The jury, composed of a talking tree, a ghost horse, and a sentient puddle, stared in mild existential dread.

The prosecution (also Loki) dramatically adjusted his robes. "Ladies, gentlemen, and others, today we put Loki on trial not just for his crimes... but for his vibes."

Defence Loki (also Loki) scoffed. "Objection! That's incredibly vague."

Judge: "Sustained. But continue, I'm mildly entertained."

The evidence included:
• A flaming duck.
• A musical number.
• A squirrel witness who refused to speak without a glitter mic.

The trial lasted three days. On day two, someone summoned Odin as a surprise witness. Odin refused to testify without his coffee.

On day three, Loki cross-examined himself. The court transcripts read: "Snark, mischief, excessive self-awareness."

In the end, the jury ruled in favor of 'whoever brought the snacks.' Loki won.

Loki always wins. Even when he's losing.

Court adjourned to applause and one dramatic fainting goat.

No one remembers what the original charges were.

The Girl Who Said No to the Moon

They came to her window on the third night of her seventh year.

Whispers on the wind, silver-laced and full of promise. The kind of voice that smelled like moonflowers and sounded like the dream you forgot upon waking.

"Come with us," the moon said.

"No," said the girl.

It wasn't defiance. It wasn't fear. It was simply a truth she knew in her bones: she was not meant to follow.

The moon blinked or at least seemed to. No one had ever said no before.

The stars giggled nervously. A comet reversed direction just to make sure it heard correctly.

"No?" asked the night.

"No," the girl repeated, swinging her legs from the windowsill.

The moon tried again. "But we will show you galaxies. Teach you to name the dark. Wrap you in light and crown you with stories."

"I don't want to be a story," she said. "I want to live."

And that broke something.

In the distance, a prophecy fell off a shelf. Somewhere, a seer fainted. The river of fate paused its flow.

The girl turned away from the window and went back to bed. Her stuffed bear welcomed her with silent understanding.

The stars did not forget her.

Years later, they watched her grow into a woman who walked boldly, who defied oracles, who rewrote destinies.

But some nights, when the sky is especially still, the moon still waits outside her window.

Just in case she changes her mind.

The Cradle and the Sea

A sailor discovers a starlit realm hidden beneath the waves.

The sea was never quiet. It hummed with memory, whispered with longing, and called to those who knew how to listen.

She was one of them. A sailor by trade, but something else by blood. Her grandmother had told her stories as a child; tales of realms that shimmered beneath the tides, of stars that drowned to become pearls, and of gates that opened only under moonlight.

So when the storm came, she didn't steer away.

She followed it.

Lightning cracked. Waves rose like ancient gods. The crew screamed, but she smiled.

At the eye of the storm, where time stilled and water glittered with starlight, she found it: a spiral of light descending beneath the waves.

No air. No ship. Just her.

And the realm that had always whispered her name.

When she returned, days or decades later, no one

was quite sure, she carried salt in her hair, a map in her skin, and a pearl that pulsed with the tide.

She never spoke of what she saw.

But on quiet nights, she would sing lullabies in a language older than time.

And the sea would answer.

The Ash and the Antlers

A memory from Kaelun's past, before Aurelya.

The forest was quiet in the way that only ancient places can be, where even the wind treads lightly, and time forgets itself.

Kaelun stood at the edge of a clearing, his antlers catching the last of the starlight. Before Aurelya. Before prophecy. Before everything that fractured him into more than just a sentinel.

He remembered the song.

It came on fog-bound nights like this, drifting through the trees on notes no mortal could replicate. It was the sound of memory without sorrow, hope without future. And it always led him here.

To her.

She wore silence like a cloak, bark braiding through her hair, and moss beneath her feet. Her eyes were galaxies buried in soil.

"You're late," she said, with the fondness of centuries.
"I was guarding the edges again," Kaelun replied.

"And who guards your edges?"

He never had an answer. Not then. Not ever.

The stag beside him, not a mount, but a companion, lowered its head in greeting to the woman who once made the stars pause. She ran a hand across its brow, then looked up at Kaelun with something that might have been sorrow... or might have been a warning.

"The threads are thinning," she said.

Kaelun nodded. "I know."

"Then why are you here?"

His reply came without thought. "Because I needed to remember who I was before I broke."

And for a moment, just one, he did.

He stepped forward.

The clearing accepted him.
The starlight held its breath.

A Flame Without a Name

A child born in the Realm of Flame remembers. The flames did not burn her.

They whispered.

From the moment she opened her eyes, the fire spoke in crackles and hisses, telling stories no one else could hear. The other children cried when the sparks came close. She reached out and giggled as they danced across her fingers.

She was unnamed, unclaimed, a foundling left at the edge of the Ember Wells. The monks of the Flamewatch took her in, muttering about prophecy and trouble, but fed her all the same.

They called her Emberling.

By seven, she could walk across coals without a wince. By ten, the torches bowed toward her when she entered the room. By twelve, the High Flamekeeper warned the council: "The fire is listening to her. And worse, it seems to like her."

But the girl had no desire for power. Only for stories.

She spent her nights in the archives, coaxing half-burned scrolls back to life with careful heat and breath. The fire never consumed when she asked nicely.

And then, one night, it answered her.

In the deepest chamber, where the oldest flame burned, the First Spark, she whispered, "Who am I?"

The fire flared. And from it stepped a vision of a woman crowned in smoke and embers.

"My child," the figure said, "you were not left behind. You were sent ahead."

The flames pulsed with memory. And the girl, no longer just Emberling, knew she had a name. One the fire would keep safe until it was time.

A flame without a name. For now.

The Goat Who Would Be King

A tale of Thor's chicken-goat hybrid, destiny, and a very unqualified squirrel advisor.

Once upon a time, because that's the only way these things ever start, there lived a goat.

Except, it wasn't just a goat.

It had feathers.

And talons.

And an attitude that could only be described as "mildly possessed by chaos."

Thor, in one of his less lucid moments (which was saying something), had decided to improve on nature by combining his Favourite animals: a goat and a chicken. The result was "Cluckles," a creature that defied taxonomy, decency, and basic laws of aviation.

Cluckles had dreams.

He also had a squirrel named Jibbers as his royal advisor.
Jibbers had no qualifications for this job, unless

you counted the ability to yell "Viva la revolution!" while launching himself from chandeliers.

Thor, of course, thought this was all perfectly reasonable.

"It's about legacy!" Thor bellowed, draping Cluckles in a tiny cape stitched with runes of questionable translation. "The realms need a new leader! A new hope! A slightly confused barnyard dictator with feathers!"

Loki stared at the scene.

Then at Cluckles.

Then at Jibbers, who was now gnawing through a map of the nine realms.

"I'm not even surprised," Loki muttered. "I'm just... tired."

But the chaos couldn't be stopped.

Cluckles took to the campaign trail, which was less a trail and more a series of loud declarations made from rooftops.
Jibbers handled PR.

Posters appeared.

"Vote Cluckles: Because He Said So!"

"Feathers. Fury. Freedom."

"Peck the System."

The other realms watched in stunned silence.

And then, somehow, it worked.

Cluckles became King of Realm Three and instituted new laws, including mandatory midday naps, all-you-can-eat bug buffets, and formal tiaras for all goats.

Jibbers became Minister of Mischief and was last seen negotiating trade deals using acorns and interpretive dance.

Thor wept tears of pride.

Odin wept tears of confusion.

And Loki, ever the realist, just opened a betting pool on how long the monarchy would last.
The answer: longer than expected.

And so, dear reader, if you ever hear distant squawking followed by the declaration of "All Hail King Cluckles!", just bow.

It's safer that way.

Whispers in the Glass

A mirror learns what it means to reflect.

The mirror had seen centuries.

It had reflected queens at their cruellest, lovers at their most fragile, and children who didn't yet know what they feared. But never once, in all that time, had anyone asked the mirror how it felt.

Until her.

Aurelya didn't speak as she entered the chamber of glass. She didn't need to. Her eyes were full of a thousand unspoken stories. The mirror waited, humming with old enchantments, its surface shimmering faintly in her presence.

"You've seen everything," she finally whispered.

The mirror pulsed.

"Yes," it replied, though its voice came not with sound, but with memory. It showed her a flash of laughter, a scream, a soft lullaby in a foreign tongue.
"I need to know what's true," she said.

The mirror didn't lie. But it didn't soften either.

And as Aurelya looked into it, into herself, it showed her every mask she had worn, every moment she had flinched, every truth she had swallowed to protect someone else.

She did not cry.

But she did nod.

"Thank you," she said.

And for the first time in centuries... the mirror felt seen.

The Garden Fracture

A story from the realm Aurelya never visited, and why.

There are realms that demand attention, all
storm and shadow, glory and gold.
And then there are realms like the Garden.

The Garden didn't roar for recognition.
It didn't hunger to be remembered.
It simply… grew.

Once, long ago, Aurelya stood at its edge. One
foot in, one foot out.
But something stopped her.
Not fear.
Not doubt.
Something older.

A whisper not from the trees, but from her own
bones:
"Not yet."

No maps marked it.
No names held it.
And yet, the Garden waited, not with longing, but
with certainty.

Those who enter the Garden do not return
unchanged.
And those who avoid it?
They carry questions that bloom in silence.

This is not Aurelya's story.
Not yet.

But the Garden remembers.
And one day, it will call again.

The Masked and the Missing

One of the Witnesses breaks their vow of silence.

In the forgotten folds of the tenth realm, where silence is law and memory itself treads lightly, one of the Witnesses stirred.

They had no name, only a mask etched with truths no one wanted to see.

They were never meant to speak.

But tonight, the stars flickered like nervous secrets, and the realm, stitched together by silence, trembled.

Aurelya arrived without warning. Her footsteps didn't echo, but the weight of her presence did. She bowed respectfully to the robed figure sitting in the temple's shadow.

"I'm not here to ask," she said. "I'm here to remember."

The Witness didn't nod. Didn't speak. But their hand moved, slowly, to remove the mask.

Underneath, there was no face. Just light. Flickering. Fractured. Familiar.

And then, like the unravelling of a forgotten thread, the Witness began to speak.

They told of the first fracture in the realms.

Of a love so bright it could only exist in shadow.

Of a child who should never have lived, and yet burned brighter than fate allowed.

Of names erased from scrolls, and of one name whispered in defiance.

"Aurelya."

When they finished, the temple shook. Their vow was broken. The realm would remember.

And the stars, those ever-watching witnesses, wept softly in gratitude.

Meanwhile, in the Realm of Therapy

The realms go to group counselling.
Chad the Goblin Life Coach returns.

Location: A folding chair circle in a suspiciously
cozy cave.
Chad the Goblin Life Coach adjusted his lopsided
spectacles and clicked his pen. "Okay, everyone,
remember the rules: no interrupting, no
incinerating your fellow attendees, and if you're
going to shapeshift mid-share, please announce
it for the transcript."

Present today:
• Thor (confused why he's here, brought snacks
anyway)
• Loki (already lying on the chaise lounge,
uninvited)
• A Sobbing Mirror (from Realm of Reflection)
• Gerald (still in a hoodie, mumbling about the
'unfairness of it all')
• A tree that may or may not be sentient (but has
excellent posture)
• Aurelya (trying to vanish into her chair)

Chad clapped. "Let's begin! Who wants to share
their progress since last session?"

Thor raised a hand. "I didn't smash anything this
week. Just... cracked. A mug. Emotionally."

Loki rolled his eyes. "I summoned a phoenix to
light my inner fire. It set my curtains on fire
instead, but still counts."
The mirror wept quietly. Chad handed it a box of
tissues.

Gerald mumbled, "I wrote a poem. It rhymed
with betrayal. A lot."
The tree rustled, which Chad took as agreement.

"Wonderful progress!" Chad beamed. "Now, let's
try group trust falls. Thor, you're up first."
The session ended with laughter, mild injuries,
and a group agreement to try hot yoga next time,
except the tree, who refused to bend.

Chad's closing words: "Healing is messy. So is
group therapy. But at least no one summoned a
kraken this week. That's growth."

A Note from the Realms

Collected Post-Performance Reflections from Those You Survived

Loki

Stop reading this. You're emotionally compromised. That means I did my job. Also, I demand a standing ovation and a catered exit.

Nutters McFluff

Theatre changed me. I still chew stage curtains in my sleep. If you find a peanut under your pillow, I've been there. You're welcome.

P.S. Tell Gerald I'm not giving back the emotional support tiara.

Aurelya

I came here for answers. I left with raccoons, interpretive dance trauma, and a dragon who insists he's not emotionally invested. So... thank you, I think?

Sir Crumbs

No comment. My lawyer (a goose with anger issues) advised silence. But if you find tap shoes with glitter stuck to the laces, that's my signature.

Respect the sparkle.

Clarence
I didn't mean to speed-date the sea witch. She
ordered for me. It was soup. I have regrets.
Still single. Still majestic.

Gerald
Thank you for coming to my live crying circle.
We raise our emotional support juice boxes to
you. I'm proud of us. We made it weird, but we
made it.
You're seen. You're valid. You're not alone.

Chad the Goblin Life Coach
If you've read this far, you've clearly been
through some things. You're welcome at any
group therapy bonfire in Realm 6. First
marshmallows free.

Realm seal

About the Author

Holly Symons once tried to write a "normal" fantasy novel. It lasted three sentences.

Since then, she's been wrangling talking lions, emotionally unavailable side characters, rogue scrolls, and at least three gods who refuse to follow their plotlines. When not rewriting the Realms (again), she can be found sipping tea, staring dramatically out windows, and whispering "just one more chapter" to characters who stopped listening seven books ago.

She believes in epic quests, emotional chaos, and that punctuation marks have feelings too.